# Caught by Him

Tammy Mannersly

Caught By Him
Copyright © 2017 Tammy Mannersly
All rights reserved.

ISBN: (ebook) 978-1-953335-02-9
(print) 978-1-953335-03-6

Inkspell Publishing
207 Moonglow Circle #101
Murrells Inlet, SC 29576

Cover art By The Write Designer

## OTHER BOOKS BY TAMMY MANNERSLY

TAMMY MANNERSLY

# DEDICATION

To Fiona, Kristina and Tess
Thanks for your friendship, love and encouragement.

TAMMY MANNERSLY

# CHAPTER ONE

Simple words didn't make sense anymore. Brody Nash paced, the same thing he'd been doing for the last half hour, and read the same line of his new script over and over again. He'd tried it so many ways: enthusiastic, cunning, smug, even perplexed. Nothing was working. The personal direction in parentheses below his character's capitalized name read: *fighting back a smirk*.

*What the hell did that mean?*

In the warm glow of the overhead lighting, his cocoa-brown eyes scanned the line again.

"Life is only worth living if you've got something to lose." This time there wasn't any emotion in his voice.

He'd gone beyond feeling any connection to the character – not that he'd had much to begin with anyway. Mike Karver, or 'The Wolf' as he was known to his associates in the story, was a laidback grifter, someone who rolled with the punches and grasped onto the rollercoaster of life with both hands. Brody Nash was the total opposite. He was a planner, someone who enjoyed organizing his things, his house, and his life. He liked to think everything through before committing and always had a plan B if things didn't work out as expected.

1

Although Brody was resilient and determined, a bit like his new character, he could also be self-deprecating and anxious – the scars of a Hollywood career which had peaked early in life. He knew there was no real reason for the apprehension he'd developed. After ten years in the spotlight, he was still the go-to leading man for many different roles, had numerous movies debuting each year, and found himself nominated for annual awards. But he was starting to feel as though something was missing inside of him and it had him questioning everything – including himself.

"What am I doing?" Brody tossed the script onto the cream-colored, three-seater sofa beside him and then ran a hand through his thick, dark chocolate curls.

He glanced around the living room. It was magnificent – spacious, contemporary, clean – just like the rest of the mansion. He'd bought the Point Piper property a few years back when he'd decided he wanted to have a base in Australia, near his hometown of Sydney. He even oversaw the refurbishments, making sure everything made it the home he'd always wanted. Yet he'd never had a chance to enjoy his new residence and instead, was right back on the next flight to Los Angeles to prepare for another blockbuster.

It was the main reason the house was so damned spotless as though it was blatantly obvious it had been uninhabited. He'd only arrived in town the night before. He hadn't yet had a chance to make it look lived in and boy, did he plan to. He'd told his brilliant agent, Kevin Rhineer, he needed a few months of character building before he'd feel comfortable to start filming and his marvelous agent had wrangled a deal with the director. Brody would get three months before shooting as long as he committed to the planned sequel. With everything agreed upon and signed, he was really looking forward to time to focus, to catch his breath and find his feet. In the movie industry, things moved very quickly, sometimes too fast. Brody had felt as though he'd been hurtling at light-speed ever since his star-making role in the action flick *Deadly Mission* when he was eighteen. He really needed this time, and hoped he could come up with the confidence to play this new character before his time was up.

With a sigh, Brody strode toward the closed French doors which overlooked the sheltered bay, flowing out into Sydney Harbor. It was after ten on a Monday night and the only light remaining came from a few boats drifting on the thick, black water, a couple of houses across the distance of the bay and the security light on his neighbor's private pontoon below.

An unfamiliar boat moored at the platform drew his attention. Illuminated by the warm glow of the outdoor floodlight, Brody could see an old-fashioned houseboat with a quaint-looking porch at either end and ladder access to the flat-topped roof. Although there hadn't been a boat of any kind moored when he'd arrived yesterday, he definitely hadn't expected his neighbor, the owner of a mansion which rivaled his own in expense and grandeur, to own such a shabby looking vessel. Then he saw the shadowy silhouette.

A person moving in the darkness, wearing dark clothes and carrying some sort of duffle bag, had adrenalin shooting through him. The figure jumped from the boat to the pontoon.

*What was happening? Was this person a visitor or a trespasser?*

Brody's heart raced. The individual headed up the pontoon, toward the connecting jetty and the grassy verge in front of his neighbor's home, shadows devoured their image as they disappeared.

A fierce oath left Brody's lips in a mixture of fear and irritation. His body froze in place, not quite prepared to go fight some stranger in the middle of the night, but absolutely furious someone had dared to disturb his peaceful solitude.

Knowing he had only minutes to make his decision,

Brody weighed his options. A twenty-four-hour security service roamed the local streets and could be hailed with one quick call, so could the police. He could call his neighbor to warn them about the impending danger – or touching reunion, he reminded himself, depending on the shadowy figure's intentions – or intercept the dark-clothed person himself. There was sure to be a baseball bat, heavy lamp-stand or handy broom nearby he could use as backup. Or, lastly, he could forget about it completely and pretend he never saw anything.

The Brody Nash who liked to stay out of trouble and mind his own business would have taken option one, two or five. The situation had nothing at all to do with him and the professionals were better equipped to deal with an intruder. But this Brody, the one who was trying to become more daring like the role he'd committed to play, was actually considering taking option four. *God help him.*

Spinning around, Brody searched the living room for something he could use as a weapon – if only for intimidation purposes.

*

The gate was locked and none of the keys she'd been given would open it. Was there anything else that could go wrong in Willabelle Stone's life today? She didn't think so, but there was still an hour or so to go before it ended, so who knew?

Willa tossed her black duffle bag over the top of the perilous wrought iron spires and prepared to do the same thing with her own body. She was lucky the gate was chest high and without a security alarm, otherwise she'd have given up on the spot.

When her grandfather, Murray, had called her earlier to let her know he desperately needed someone to housesit for him last minute, she'd wanted nothing more than to say 'sorry, no can do'. Yet, she'd known she couldn't. She owed him more than just the usual family obligation. Her business, her life, even her home, wouldn't have been the same without him. So, she'd said yes.

Apparently, his live-in housekeeper had been notified of a family emergency in Adelaide and wouldn't be back for a few weeks. With Murray currently working in California for the next couple of months and the rest of her rather small family busy with their own obligations during that time, Willa had been his last and only option. She'd known being his final choice hadn't insinuated in any way he hadn't wanted to turn to her. No, in fact, it was quite the opposite.

Being the only grandchild, Willa had always been close with her beloved grandfather. But Murray understood her well enough to know that she needed her own space. He'd often told her she was a free spirit like her grandmother, the incredible woman she'd been named after. She'd never known her, having lost her namesake to cancer when Willa was only three. Her grandfather realized that asking her to tie herself down to a place, would grate on her every nerve. He knew she enjoyed her freedom and yearned for the spontaneity in life. But he had no one else to ask. And for him, she'd do almost anything.

Willa mentally chided herself as she climbed the cold, wrought iron gate. If she'd made a bigger effort to come earlier, then maybe she could have made it to the house before night had fallen. But she hadn't been that organized, she was *never* that organized. Things kept getting in the way, and now it was nearly midnight – or close to – and she was attempting to climb over a fence. She was just grateful she had dressed sensibly for the occasion in stretchy black tights, an old indigo hoodie and dirty navy trainers. At least if she fell and broke her butt – and her clothes ended up in bloodied tatters – she wouldn't be ruining anything nice or expensive.

Realistically, she should've been blaming Hayden for her lateness. If her ex-boyfriend, the preppy, privileged yacht owner and sole heir to the Montfort fortune, had just taken her *no* as the rejection she'd meant it to be, then she'd have signed all the necessary paperwork and been out of the marina in decent time. Yet, for some reason, he still thought they had something and deserved to have a say in her life, even though it was no longer any of his business and it hadn't been for nearly two years now. She'd survived five years in his needy, suffocating embrace and even though she knew her father helped fan the flames of Hayden's hope, she had absolutely no intention of returning to the stifling relationship. She'd thought turning down his proposal of marriage would have clinched the deal, but it had done the opposite. Maybe this time away and the distance would give Hayden some space to re-evaluate things and realize his idea of them was only in his own head.

As Willa hitched a long leg over the sharp spires and made a risky attempt to straddle the gate, she was distracted by a flicker of light on the path below. Intrigued rather than fearful, she glanced up and saw a tall, dark figure hurrying toward her, protected partly from her view by the blinding glow of a flashlight.

"Stop!" It was a stern, masculine yell, one which would've sounded a lot more dangerous had their hand, and therefore the light, not been shaking. "Don't even think about making another move."

Miffed, both by the interruption and the order, Willa grimaced. Just how was she supposed to freeze with her delicate feminine bits above the sharp point of an iron spire?

Prepared to ignore the intruder's demand, assuming she was probably safer on the other side of the fence anyway, Willa made a move to swing her other leg up and over.

"I said freeze!" Once again it was a gruff instruction, one which was made the slightest bit less intimidating by the wavering lilt on the final word.

Willa paused once more in her precarious position,

with her left foot balanced on a high horizontal bar, and steadied her weight just enough for her to remain perched in place for a little longer.

"Actually, you said *stop* before, not freeze." She hadn't meant for it to sound so snarky.

Silence answered her as though he was processing her response and then the dark, male figure inched forward.

"I don't think you're in any position to be making digs at my choice of commands." His deep voice had lost the nervous quiver and now sounded seductive, velvety even, except for the tinge of irritation in his tone.

Willa couldn't find a reason to argue. The flashlight-wielding intruder had a good point. She wasn't in the easiest spot to make a quick escape. She opened her mouth to concede defeat. She was even willing to start begging for the opportunity to remove her precious lady parts from the danger of the spire below. But then the shadow-covered stranger lowered the flashlight just enough for her to see what he was holding in his other hand: a long metal pole attached to a blue-netted leaf rake, like one you'd use to scoop debris from the surface of a pool.

Suddenly, Willa didn't know whether to laugh or scream. What had he been planning to do with it? Catch her like a butterfly? Or maybe he'd just come from cleaning the pool next door? The image had a laugh tickling the back of her throat but she held it in.

As though sensing her humorous take on the situation, the tall, dark stranger waved the pole toward her in warning and Willa wobbled the tiniest bit on her perch. Instinct had her attempting to raise both hands in obvious surrender, but she quickly realized how precarious her situation was. With one hand in the air, she held her flat palm up and out toward him.

"Whoa there, neighborhood watch!" It was all the capitulation she could manage.

"Okay, now that you're taking me seriously," he told her in that deep, silky voice, "I think it's time you remove yourself from that gate."

Willa tilted her head. Surely, which *side* of the gate was still up for negotiation, and she was willing to bet, she'd still be much safer on the side she was already heading toward than on the one with the crazed man brandishing a pool-cleaning tool.

Reluctant to wait for a more specific command, Willa made one swift movement and swung the rest of her body up and over the hazardous metal spires. When she landed, surprisingly gracefully, on the cement tiles with a light thud, she heard the urgent footsteps of the stranger hurrying toward her.

"Do you have a habit of doing the opposite of what you're told?" His voice had lost any remaining edge to it and now sounded exasperated.

Pleased with herself, Willa shrugged without offering him another glance and bent to pick up her black duffle bag. "Sometimes."

"I doubt you'll be sounding so glib when the security service gets here," he growled.

Willa spun to face him, heat burned her cheeks. "You called security?"

That was all she needed. If she thought it had already been a long night, it was about to get worse.

She strode back to him, about to scold him for his stupidity, when he lowered the flashlight. As her eyes adjusted to the dark, she managed to get her first good glimpse of the stubborn man who'd made her night memorable for all the wrong reasons.

His features were strangely familiar and dark – gorgeous eyes and thick, black wavy hair – against the warm honey hue of his delectable skin. Stubble shadowed his square jaw and strong neck, which led her gaze further down to his broad shoulders and the strong muscles of his arms and chest encased in a midnight blue shirt. The tight material ended just above his slate grey track pants, giving her a tempting view of golden skin and a soft trail of dark hair leading down to a sizeable bulge below. At the sight of his huge feet in black flip-flops, Willa had a moment of mental calculation – considering the big hands, big feet theory – before realizing she'd taken a very long minute to check him out.

When her gaze met his again, over the deadly, decorative spears atop the gate, it became obvious he'd just finished doing the same thing to her.

Willa offered him a haughty smirk. "Maybe if you'd been a little nicer to me, I would've dropped down on your side and this all could've gone a very different way."

A dark eyebrow shot up at her insinuation. "Sorry, but I don't date criminals."

Willa's jaw dropped as her free hand went to her chest protectively, and then she smiled. "Who said anything about dating?"

Spinning on her heel, she flipped the duffle bag's strap over her shoulder and headed up the cement tiles toward the back door of her grandfather's mansion.

"Wait!" The tall, dark and handsome stranger's voice rang out behind her.

Was that a hint of worry raising his pitch a little higher? She really hoped so.

"What about the security service? They'll catch you if you break into that property."

Willa frowned and glanced back at him. "Break in, yes. But, I have the key."

She snatched the cluster of keys from where they'd been clipped to the side of the duffle bag and waved the shiny objects at him. She could've sworn she heard a muffled curse from his direction. Ignoring it and the magnetic appeal of his complete hotness, she turned back and managed to make it to the door.

As she inserted the key neatly labelled *rear door*, she turned her head to look back down the path in his direction. He was still staring at her, looking over the gate, his hands wrapped around the iron bars. The flashlight and leaf rake lay at his feet. She smiled and thought she saw a small smile in return.

"In case you'd forgotten to ask between threats and insults," she told him sweetly. "My name is Willa Stone and my grandfather owns this place."

There was a flash of white as he grinned bashfully. "Not a burglar then?"

Willa chuckled as she opened the door. "Only of hearts," she teased.

Then she stepped inside and closed the door behind her.

# CHAPTER TWO

He hadn't told her his name. It was the one thing about the whole debacle which Brody regretted the most. Even after spending two hours trying to convince the security service guys to leave – well, twenty minutes of explaining and the rest answering questions about his movie star career and signing their personal effects – he still hadn't been able to shake the gut-wrenching mistake. A few days had passed and he'd only managed a glimpse of her. He'd expected the feeling to ebb away, yet it haunted him.

She'd even given him an opening by telling him hers – *Willa Stone*. The name sounded so familiar, but Brody was betting that could've had something to do with the fact that it was beautiful, just like her.

He'd been a goner as soon as he'd seen her face, those big amber eyes framed with long dark lashes, her peaches and cream skin, the neat little nose and those lush lips which seemed to curve ever so slightly at the sides as though she was permanently smiling or laughing at some cheeky insider joke. Her long golden hair was streaked with caramel and had curled sneakily from beneath the dark purple of her hooded sweater, which revealed just enough of her shape to suggest that her body was a sexy wonderland. She appeared to have full, feminine curves in all the right places, long, slender limbs – and, *oh dear God,* her ass, the perfect roundness in her snug, black tights had made his groin ache and his fingers itch. He longed to touch her, to hold her, all of her. There was something about Willa Stone which was almost irresistible, something Brody hadn't experienced before and something he wanted to get to the bottom of – literally.

"So, can I put you down for nine tomorrow morning?" Carmody Hewitt didn't glance up from her smartphone as she asked him for clarification. "Tim's rather prompt, so I'd be ready to go a little earlier."

Brody shook away his thoughts of Willa, then hooked his thumbs through the belt loops of his blue jeans and moved from the picture window back toward the sleek, white marble island in the kitchen.

"Sorry. What?"

He'd gathered the gist of what had been said, but didn't want to commit to something without hearing all the details clearly. It was something he'd learned from his agent and a total must when it came to contracts.

From where she casually leaned her slim hip against the countertop, Carmody glanced up at him, offering him a compassionate smile. She looked as flawless as she had when he'd met her the night before, in her designer dress and matching heels, with her makeup precise and her immaculate bob of dark hair.

Kevin, Brody's agent, had arranged for Brody to have a reliable personal assistant on hand to organize all of his necessities: grocery deliveries, personal trainer appointments, PR prerequisites and the like. But Brody had expected a Kevin-clone, as his agent and long-time friend was often very particular about who he let organize the lives of his A-list stars. Then Carmody – or *Carm* as she'd instructed him to call her – had arrived and he'd been surprised, before realizing that just because she didn't have Kevin's Tom Ford suit and salt and pepper hair, it didn't mean she wasn't like him in many other respects.

"Brody." She purred, letting her tongue roll over his name, as she rounded the kitchen island toward him. "Kevin told me how hard you've been working, trying to immerse yourself into this new character. If it's too much to start your new personal training program tomorrow, I can organize for Tim to come over on Sunday?"

Brody shook his head. "No, tomorrow's fine. I'm just a bit distracted this morning."

He raised a hand and ran his fingers through his hair.

A strange feeling built in his gut. It had been niggling there since Monday night. Something between nerves of excitement and a heavy weight of fear. Initially, he'd put it down to the worry regarding his new role but as time had progressed, he'd started to think it had something more to do with Willa and the opportunity he'd missed.

Carmody took a step closer to him then reached out to cup his cheek. The physical touch surprised Brody and he flinched slightly, before accepting the reassuring gesture.

"Don't push yourself too hard, honey. You don't want to burn out before the next blockbuster." She dropped her manicured hand from his face and then patted him on the chest. "If you need a break, you just let me know. I can wipe your schedule clean like that." She clicked her elegant fingers.

He forced a smile. "Thanks, Carm, but I think I'm good for the moment."

A perfect brown eyebrow arched in response and then she grinned at him, all wide and pearly white. "Great. Then nine a.m. tomorrow it is."

Carmody's attention returned to her smartphone as she stepped around him and walked out of the kitchen toward the corridor. Brody followed her toward the mansion's front door.

"You're in a great neighborhood," Carmody commented over her shoulder, "and in good company. You've got a famous director as a neighbor. Old school, but brilliant. I can try to contact him if you'd like introductions?"

Brody felt like sighing. A few years ago, he would have jumped at the opportunity. He'd been riding the rollercoaster of fame back then and had taken advantage of every meet and greet presented to him, but now he needed to focus on this new role. Offers often flowed in to his agent, so there was no longer any need to put the same exhausting energy into networking.

"I appreciate the thought," Brody explained, "but I'll have to take a raincheck."

Carmody shrugged and glanced back at him. "Let me know if you change your mind. It's a great opportunity."

As the carpet of the corridor turned to the white tiles of the front entry, Carmody finally lowered her phone and looked up at Brody, her wide grin fixing back in place.

"Okay," she breathed. "Your grocery delivery has been set for Mondays, weekly from now on, but we can add additional deliveries if necessary. I'll have some more papers for you to sign before the end of the week and further information regarding that magazine spread Esquire wants to do. You've got Tim tomorrow at nine, then on Sunday at four. I've put it in your calendar, but I'll be in touch as often as possible."

When she finally took a breath, Brody nodded. Then she opened the front door and stepped outside into the gated courtyard beyond. Still barefooted, Brody followed her onto the paved driveway, watching as her grin never faltered. He couldn't tell if her constant state of glee was sincere, just put on for the sake of professionalism, or as phony as hell. Kevin was often the same but Brody had seen behind the mask enough to know when it was a real smile or not. He didn't know Carmody Hewitt well enough yet and wasn't sure he really wanted to.

Just as Brody was starting to feel relief in knowing that Carmody would be leaving him in peace very soon, she turned to face him again. Her pristine smile plastered in place.

"Remember the maid service comes on Tuesdays at ten, so don't stress yourself over the washing up," she told him before stepping a little closer. "And if you ever want company or need help *relaxing*, just give me a call. I've been told I'm *very useful* to have around."

It was not difficult to miss her suggestion. Just the way she'd drawn out certain words had been enough for Brody to wonder whether Kevin had known about this added 'benefit' when he'd hired her. He'd nagged Brody about getting some action, concerned his career goals were putting love, or at least sex, on the backburner. Kevin had made a point to remind him he was a big-shot-movie-star now and could get just about any woman he wanted, maybe even more than one at once, but Brody just hadn't been interested. He'd had a few on-set romances with his single leading ladies over the years, but they'd never gone anywhere and he'd become convinced women seemed to like him for the characters he played, rather than for who he really was. That had turned him off dating co-stars and as for women of another variety, he didn't often meet them or didn't like them much when he did.

Seemingly pleased with the reaction Brody had given her, Carmody winked at him and then headed toward the black Jaguar convertible parked on the drive before them.

"Guess I'll be seeing you again soon," she called out over her shoulder as she waved one graceful hand.

Out of habit and ingrained politeness, Brody answered Carmody's wave with one of his own. Once in the car, she slipped on her sunglasses, offered him another bold grin, and then drove the convertible slowly toward the grand, eight-foot tall entry gate which shielded them from the outside world. As the huge wooden gates coasted open, Brody noticed a familiar face jogging down the street and moved closer to the end of the driveway.

With her golden hair in a high ponytail, which swayed sexily with each step, her kissable skin glistening and her alluring curves encased in brightly colored Lycra, Willa looked as though she'd just jumped off the cover of a women's fitness magazine. As she saw him, her face brightened and she smiled with obvious delight.

"Hi there, neighbor," she called out to him, capturing Carmody's attention as she drove past her and out onto the road.

Even though the Jaguar didn't stop, Brody took note of Carmody's look of distaste before she sped away.

"Morning." He smiled his biggest grin at Willa.

Willa ran the last few steps onto his driveway and then slowed her pace to a walk. "Guess the maid service has come and gone." She offered him a smirk as she tilted her head in the direction of the convertible.

Brody chuckled and then opened his mouth to correct her, but she quickly cut him off.

"Sorry. Girlfriend." She propped her hands on her hips. "I should've realized. It makes sense a guy like you would be taken."

Intrigued, his gaze narrowed on hers. "A guy like me? What does that mean?"

"You know," she began to explain matter-of-factly with a nod in his direction, "a guy who cleans his own pool and uses the same pool-cleaning gizmo to protect the neighborhood."

"Oh, that kind of guy." He laughed. "You make me sound a B-squad superhero."

She raised her blonde eyebrows as though agreeing with his suggestion and then shrugged. "If the B-squad superhero costume fits…"

Brody laughed again, before offering her a more serious expression. "She's not my girlfriend."

As the huge entry gates closed, Brody and Willa moved instinctually out of the way, walking further down the driveway toward Brody's mansion.

Willa's amber gaze never left his. "Fiancé? Wife? Polyamorous partner?"

Laughing with surprise, Brody shook his head. "No, none of those."

Willa eyed him cautiously and then seemed to accept his answer. "These days you can never be too careful." As she shrugged again, the contagious smile he was so fond of returned. "So, Mr. B-squad superhero, are you going to tell me your name? Or, at the very least, your alter ego?"

Very pleased to be able to have a second chance at an introduction with a woman who was quickly becoming the woman of his dreams, Brody couldn't help but play along. Humorously, he narrowed his gaze and leaned closer to her. "Promise you won't tell the reporters at the *Daily Planet*?"

She raised a hand and held up three fingers. "Girl Scout's honor."

"Well, then," Brody said, holding out a hand in greeting, "the name's Brody Nash."

As she slipped a soft hand into his, a jolt of electricity shot up his arm, igniting a further spark of desire in his groin and his heart.

"Now, that's a name I've definitely seen on the big screen," she told him with a knowing smile. "I should've guessed. *Movie star* is written all over those fabulous features."

He felt his eyes widen at the compliment. "You think I'm fabulous?"

Willa pulled her hand free from his. Brody felt the loss of their physical connection. She narrowed her beautiful amber eyes and her full lips curled in a mischievous smile.

"Geez, what is it with you actors and the need to have society's constant validation? Just look in a mirror once and a while, why don't you?"

He smirked. "I hope you know I'm taking all your trash talk as a compliment."

She rolled her eyes, her expression vibrant. "Fine. I guess you have to feed the ego."

He laughed and felt the unsettling feeling in his gut

again. *Was it fear? Excitement? Nervous butterflies?*

"What are you doing right now?" The words just burst out of him.

She tilted her head and raised a blonde eyebrow. "Talking to you."

Brody laughed again. "No. After this. Do you have plans?"

Her grin widened. "Why Captain Famous – that's your new superhero name by the way – are you asking me to spend time with you?"

With a chuckle, he nodded. "If you're not too busy."

Willa stepped closer to him, leaving barely a foot of space between them and then glanced around cautiously before frowning. "Careful," she whispered, "You don't want people to think you're dating criminals now."

Brody forced his expression to become serious as he leaned closer to her, their lips almost touching. "Who said anything about dating?"

Willa smirked. "Touché."

As she lingered close, her gaze drifted down to his lips and back to his eyes. Brody struggled against his own temptations. She was so close, with just the slightest movement he could be kissing her. His whole body ached for it. He clenched his fists against the desire to reach out to her. He tried to suck in a steadying breath, but inhaled her warm, sweet scent – jasmine and a honeyed muskiness.

Even as Brody tried to fight it, lust shook through him and his willpower weakened. Willa gave him a small smile which seemed tinged with disappointment and then she retreated, giving him space he desperately didn't want. With a little shake of her head, she opened her mouth to speak.

Brody couldn't control himself any longer. Slipping an arm around her bare waist, he pulled her against him and claimed her open mouth with his own. It wasn't the gentle kiss he'd planned to start with. It was hot, wet and passionate. It was dancing tongues, deep probing and breathlessness. It was all consuming, utterly devouring as though he was trying to suck her essence, her very soul inside him.

As he'd pressed her to him, her firm curves meeting the hard line of his body, she'd made a squeak in surprise, but then relaxed into the embrace, small moans emanating from her throat as their kiss deepened. She tasted so sweet, he couldn't get enough of her, couldn't stop. One hand cupped her face, holding her to him, while the other at her waist slipped lower, over the smooth spandex of her exercise tights to grasp the lusciousness of her ass. Willa made an audible gasp against his mouth at his sudden possession of her backside. She melted further against him, her hands moving from his chest, to slip languidly around his neck. Brody groaned at her touch. He wanted more, wanted her naked underneath him as he thrust into her. He ate at her mouth, nibbling her lips, his tongue caressing hers.

Brody's hand dropped from her face to her collarbone, and grazed over her plump breast before pausing on the soft skin just beneath the Lycra of her black and magenta crop top. As his fingers moved to sneak under the snug elasticized fabric, Willa stiffened slightly and freed herself from his kiss.

"Hold it there, love thy-neighbor," she panted. "It's not that I wouldn't love for this to continue, but why don't we try it again later when I'm not all stinky and disgusting and doing my best impression of a sweaty rainbow?"

Her hand slipped from his neck to gesture at her sexy figure wrapped tightly in brightly colored spandex.

Brody's chuckle sounded more like a growl. "I don't know what you're talking about. You look—" he gazed over her and groaned. "You smell incredible."

He bent his head to kiss her again, but Willa pulled back at the last minute and giggled.

"At least, let me take a shower," she told him.

Brody smirked mischievously. "*I* have a shower."

Willa's stunning amber eyes widened and then she bit her lower lip as though she was actually considering his suggestion. It sent an ache of desire through him, his groin throbbing as he hoped for the possibility. She gazed down at his mouth and then back up into his eyes, before touching her lips softly, but briefly to his. Brody tried to catch her, lock her into another ardent kiss, but she was too quick for him. He tightened his grip on the soft skin of her side and clutched at the fullness of her ass, fearful she might pull away further. The strange feeling in his gut started again, churning and filling him with uneasiness.

"I don't want you to think I'm not easy," she flirted, her free hand returning to his chest to draw circles over the cotton of his shirt, making his skin buzz with sensitivity, "because, for the right person, I definitely am. But—" Willa gnawed at her lower lip again. "The world might know this Brody Nash character, famous movie star and friendly neighborhood superhero, but I don't and I'd like to—before we share showers."

Brody bit back a laugh. Even though Willa had made light of the situation, showing the funny side of it all, she'd said enough to have his heartstrings straining. The fact she wanted to get to know the real Brody Nash – not the one plastered on the covers of magazines, acting in movies or being interviewed on talk shows – had the unusual fluttering in his stomach building. It felt like an exhilaration that somebody actually cared enough to want to know more about him. But it also felt like terror which made him fearful of losing her.

Willa was something special, he was sure of it and he couldn't bear the thought of not having the vibrant spark of her in his life. Brody had never felt this way before. He liked the way she made him feel, the way she felt in his arms and he couldn't seem to get enough of her witty, vivacious personality. His agent, Kevin, had been right. Brody had been putting love on the backburner and, now that he'd found what he'd been looking for, he was going to hold on tight and fight to keep it.

Brody leaned forward, snuck a quick kiss from her and then smiled. "So, there's hope for shared showers in the future?"

With a giggle, Willa grinned. "Of course. When it comes to you and me, I think shared showers may become a necessity."

Brody laughed and touched his nose affectionately to hers. Their eyes met as her finger, swirled up from his chest toward his neck. Brody fought off a shiver of longing as her fingertip met his skin.

"Still keen to spend time with me sans nudity, at least for today?" She teased.

Her finger drew a tingling line along his throat and up to his jaw, where she cupped his face with her palm.

As he fought the urge to devour her mouth with his all over again, Brody offered her a nod. "I'd like to know Willa Stone better, too."

Her sexy grin broadened and she laid a gentle kiss on his chin.

"Who knows," he exhaled, his breath a little shaky as he tried to reign in his control, "maybe, by tonight, we'll know each other well enough that nudity will be back on the table?"

Willa just laughed.

# CHAPTER THREE

Willa's laptop computer buzzed at the arrival of a new email and she jumped. Mentally scolding herself, she tried to focus back on the screen and on the tasks to be completed. She was supposed to be working, not thinking about Brody and the time they'd spent together. A few days had passed in which they'd seen each other fleetingly between prior obligations and it was Tuesday, a workday, and time to concentrate on her business.

*But it wasn't happening.* With a silly grin on her face, her mind wandered.

They'd discussed everything, the extent of their lives, their hopes for the future and their dreams. As the hours passed, Willa felt their bond grow. Although it scared her, it also offered her something she'd never felt before: a desire to commit to someone.

She'd even gone into great detail about Hayden and she'd never done that with a potential lover before, but with Brody, it had felt right. What was it about the sexy movie star which had her sharing her secrets with him? Was it because he'd opened up as well?

Frankly, the night hadn't even been as intimate and sexy as she'd been hoping for. Instead, it had been mind-blowing, life changing and future altering. It should have had her running back to the bay and yet she wasn't.

With a click of the mouse, Willa opened her email, read it and typed back an answer. As she did so, her thoughts returned to the memories of her long night with Brody. It had been quite obvious when she'd arrived at his house that he'd been keen to continue from where they'd left off. The suggestion in his eyes, his body language, it had all alluded to the intimacy he wished to explore further, but he hadn't. He'd been content with just talking, and had braved nothing more than holding her hand for most of the night.

Except for the kiss goodnight when they'd finally said goodbye – and what a goodnight kiss that had been! It was as though all the raw, sexual energy which had built while they'd been together had been released when his lips had met hers. It was more than a kiss, more than an embrace. It was a sign of a promise he would most definitely make good on. It had been painful when he'd freed her from his intoxicating hold. But, they were both serious about this relationship, so they had to take things a little slower.

And they had managed to do just that over the last couple of days. Still, Willa's desires were consuming her mind.

The thump-thump of someone moving from the pontoon to her houseboat made Willa jolt. She hadn't been expecting anyone, but quickly hoped for a surprise visit from Brody. Maybe he'd already finished the work he'd had to do this morning and had come around with a lunch offer? Checking the time on her computer screen, she saw it was just past one. Taking a deep breath to help conceal her excitement, Willa stood up, straightened her sunflower yellow singlet and then ran her palms over the tough material of her denim shorts. As she moved toward the door that led to the charming, little front porch, her fingers reached to adjust the messy bun of blonde curls atop her head. With another steadying breath, she turned the handle and opened the door. As her lips parted to form a greeting, her visitor stepped into view.

"Why—" Willa glanced around flabbergasted, before continuing. "*How* are you here?"

Hayden grinned. "I wanted to see you, Wil."

He was in black swim-trunks and soaking wet. His honey blond hair was slicked back, revealing every angle of his high cheekbones and strong jaw, while his sun-kissed skin and generous muscles glistened with moisture.

Willa glared up into his midnight blue eyes as she moved to close the door in front of him. "That's not a good enough reason, Hayden."

Lightning quick, his hand shot forward and stopped her from being able to shut him out. He'd had the movement mastered. Not wanting to break the door off the hinges, Willa released it, leaving him to do what he pleased as she turned around and headed back into her sanctuary.

"Don't expect to be welcomed inside dripping wet," she told him caustically.

As she neared her computer desk, she heard the door close.

"Don't be like that, babe." His deep voice was playful. "It was a surprise. The least you can do is offer me a towel."

Willa noticed a shabby brown throw rug on the sofa nearby and threw it at him. Hayden caught it easily before it collided with his face.

"There you go," Willa told him. "It's the best I can be bothered to do unless you'd rather get your wet butt out of my house."

With a flirtatious grin, Hayden used the material to dry his skin. "I thought you might have missed me?"

Rolling her eyes, Willa slumped into her wide, leather desk chair. "It's only been a week, Hayden."

"But, I missed you," he purred, slinking toward her like a big, sulky puma.

He lay the throw rug around his neck like a bath towel and gripped onto both ends as she glared up at him.

"You can't be serious." She dismissed his comment with a wave of her hand and then tried to focus back on her work. "How did you even get here? Aren't you supposed to be in the city – working?"

Hayden shrugged and then carefully perched himself on the desktop beside her and her precious laptop. "I took the day off and thought I'd come around to see you. It was a beautiful day, so I took the yacht."

"I'm guessing that's because you knew you wouldn't make it through the front door of the house without a key." Willa moved to spit out a sardonic laugh when she suddenly realized something. "I didn't hear the yacht." She raised an eyebrow at him suspiciously.

With a smug smile, Hayden nodded. "Yeah, I anchored in the bay and swam over."

"Of course, you did." Willa's comment was more for herself than for him.

She should've realized Hayden would've found a way to see her no matter what. Willa had thought by refusing to give him unlimited access to her grandfather's house, he'd have gotten the message. Hayden had actually had the nerve to ask her to give him a key.

Willa glanced at her laptop, at the work she'd been procrastinating over, yet now would give almost anything to have the peace and solitude to continue. She could feel her annoyance building, prickling against her skin.

"I'm busy," she growled. "Either tell me what you want from me or get lost."

Hayden just laughed, an almost saccharine sound, sickly sweet with an edge of condescension. Taking the brown throw rug from around his neck, he lay it on her desk and then reached for a large glass paperweight, a clear round ball with a pink peony captured inside, and toyed with it in his hands.

"Why are you always so hot-headed, Wil? You used to

beg to spend time with me when we were teenagers, remember?"

She did, but she wasn't that girl anymore. Since she'd turned down his proposal and experienced the freedom she'd always wanted, Willa had regularly questioned how she had ever gotten involved with Hayden. Even now, she struggled to understand why. She guessed it had been a mixture of parental pressure and convenience. Her father and Hayden's had wanted them both to marry and bond the families together, like a business pairing. She was sure she had loved Hayden with a childish innocence once but she'd outgrown him and she couldn't understand why he couldn't see that.

Hayden pouted at her. "Now, all you want to do is get rid of me and work."

Willa nodded. "Exactly."

He frowned. It was a look which could rival the best sad puppy face. "You don't mean that."

Placing the paperweight back on the desk, he leaned forward and brushed a golden curl of hair from her face. Willa fought the urge to flinch away.

"You used to want to stay in bed with me all day, remember? You used to hate to go anywhere without me. You hated to leave me."

Willa's face contorted with distaste. She'd still been in her teens when they'd gotten together and Hayden had been her first. She'd felt intoxicated by the love she'd felt for him, but it had faded when she'd grown up. He wanted someone he could control and who would act accordingly, someone who matched his social scene. Even though she'd been born into a family of the same ilk, Willa had always felt like an outsider. She needed to be her own person, needed to make her own way in the world and a lot of them just didn't understand her.

She forced her expression to soften, but felt her eyebrow lift sardonically. "What do you want, Hayden?"

He chuckled again, more suggestively than before.

Lowering a hand to the arm of Willa's desk chair, he spun her to face him directly and then grabbed the other chair arm with his free hand, cutting off any easy means of escape. As Hayden leaned in closer, Willa caught the scent of his skin, the salt of the seawater and the sweet smell of sunscreen. Poised above her, his lips just a breath from hers, she knew he was trying to entice her. The problem was, she just didn't find him tempting anymore. She was over him. Her mind – and her body – didn't give a damn what he did as long as it didn't include her.

"You know what I want, Wil," he all but whispered. "What I've always wanted – you."

"Really? What a shocker." She'd tried to sound more impressed, especially after all the effort he'd put into acting all seductive, but it had come out matter-of-factly with an edge of sarcasm.

Hayden's gaze narrowed. "I think you enjoy hurting me," he told her, his deep voice straining.

Her head tilted. "I think you like hurting yourself."

With a groan of frustration, he released the chair and stood up, turning away from her, just as the sound of footsteps thudded on the deck outside. Hayden spun around. His nostrils flared.

"Are you expecting someone?" It was an accusation and one Willa was tired of.

"It's none of your business, Hayden," Willa reminded him as a flicker of trepidation had her heart beating faster.

While she hoped Brody had decided to stop by, she wasn't too enthused about having the two guys face off inside her home.

A knock at the houseboat's front door had Willa moving to stand up, but as she did so, Hayden pushed her back into the seat.

"I'll get it." His tone was aggressive and commanding.

"You don't live here," Willa snarled as she moved to push past him.

When he reached out to grab her arm, she slapped at

his hand and hurried away. Certain he was hot on her heels, instinct took over and Willa called out before Hayden could stop her from opening the door.

"Come in!" Even she could hear the lilt of panic in her voice.

"Willa?" Brody forced open the door. Concern covered his handsome expression as his gaze met hers and then found Hayden's. "I hope I'm not interrupting?"

With his tall, muscular physique encased in dark denim jeans and a black shirt, he presented an aura of toughness and handsomeness Hayden just couldn't match.

"Hi, I'm Brody. Willa's—" Brody glanced at her, eyebrows furrowing for a split-second, and then returned his attention to Hayden. "—neighbor and you are?"

"None of your business," Hayden snapped as he tried to push his way in between her and Brody.

Willa quickly pushed him back. "This—is Hayden," she explained and saw Brody nod in understanding.

"Yeah, her boyfriend, buddy," Hayden quipped. "So you can just back off."

"That's not what I've heard." Brody's voice was calm but his eyes flickered in challenge.

"What did you say?" Hayden stepped forward, fury distorting his attractive features. Willa struggled to get between the two of them.

Brody smiled slyly. "It was lovely to meet you, Hayden, but I'm afraid Willa and I already have plans for this afternoon. So, if you wouldn't mind…" With a nod of his head he gestured toward the door. "I think we'd like to have some time alone."

Relief filled Willa as she hoped Hayden might be reasonable enough to oblige, but then she saw the ferocity in his eyes.

Hayden made a noise somewhere between a scoffing and a growl. "I think you better leave."

Willa felt the menace vibrate out of him with each word.

Brody's smile remained but his lips thinned. "It was so nice of you to come by, Hayden. I'm sure Willa loved catching up, but it really is time for *you* to go." He seemed cautious in his application of sarcasm, still friendly and somewhat ignorant of the escalating animosity in the room.

Hayden snarled. "What's wrong with you, pretty boy, don't you understand English?"

It was the final straw, Willa had had enough. This was her house, Brody was her…friend. She spun and faced Hayden, the palms of her hands flat against his chest forcing him away from Brody.

"What's wrong with *you*, Hayden?" It was almost a yell. Anger flared through her, heating her cheeks and buzzing through her veins. "I'm fed up with you, with this." She motioned a hand between them. "You've been pulling this crap for nearly two years now, claiming ownership, trying to control my life. Well, guess what? If you want to remain in my life, in any kind of capacity, then you have to cut this shit out."

As he stared down at her, the fury on Hayden's face shifted and a flash of fear had his gaze narrowing.

"You don't mean that, babe." His deep voice had softened with worry.

Willa felt her expression morph with challenge. "Try me."

Hayden's midnight blue eyes searched hers as though desperate to find weakness. When he didn't find any, he swallowed. Willa watched his eyebrows furrow and his lips tighten as he glanced back over at Brody.

"Just because I'm leaving doesn't mean you've won anything, buddy."

Brody's smile in return was closed lipped and sincere. He nodded at Hayden. "Understood."

Hayden's gaze softened as it drifted back to Willa's. "You can't get rid of me that easily," he told her, his voice pained and barely above a whisper.

She sighed, partly in acknowledgement and partly in relief before he bent his head to brush his lips gently across her cheek. Willa's hands dropped from his chest as he moved past her and then paused beside Brody. The fierceness in the expression Hayden offered him seemed to subside for a moment.

"I just loved you in *Rogue Army*." He told him matter-of-factly and then shrugged. "It's my favorite film."

Brody's lips curved in an uncertain smile. "Thanks."

Hayden nodded in acceptance and then glanced back at Willa before finally exiting the houseboat.

As Willa moved toward him, Brody sighed deeply and let out a nervous chuckle.

"I don't know what I was expecting at the end there, but it definitely wasn't a compliment."

Willa laughed. "Like I told you, he might be a controlling, intrusive ex-boyfriend, but he's not a bad guy."

Brody grinned and then took her hand, pulling her closer to him. "Hi," he said sweetly as her body melted against his and his arms wrapped around her waist.

"Hello." She giggled, her arms going around his neck as she touched her lips briefly to his. "And what brings you out here?"

"I wanted to know if you had dinner plans," he said, stealing a kiss.

She raised an eyebrow curiously. "You offering to cook for me?"

He laughed. "No. I thought we could go to The Rocks and have dinner beside the Harbor Bridge."

"So fancy," she crooned and lay another kiss on his lips, her mouth molding around his more passionately this time.

Brody held her against the firmness of his body and groaned as she deepened the kiss. His tongue caressed hers as his hands slipped down to cup the roundness of her behind. Willa enjoyed the embrace, savoring the feeling of him pressed against her, his hands fondling her curves, while his lips and tongue did things to her own mouth that made her swoon before she forced herself to pull away.

"Okay," she told him breathlessly. "Even though I'd love to keep procrastinating with you—"

Brody stole another kiss and Willa had a momentary lapse of concentration before she managed to break free again.

"If we are going on a date tonight, then I should really get back to work."

Brody frowned and his cocoa-brown eyes glittered playfully. "I could always help you."

He touched his lips to the corner of her mouth, to her jaw and then dipped his head to kiss her neck. Willa sucked in a breath as her head fell back, giving him further access to the sensitive skin of her throat.

"I don't think you'd be very helpful," she moaned.

"Are you sure you don't want to find out?" His warm breath tickled over her before he nibbled at the taut skin of her neck.

Willa chuckled. "I can think of nothing I'd rather do right now," she said, finally forcing herself to straighten. "But—" she released a long sigh as she gazed up into his eyes, "I think I should take the sensible option and work now so we get to play later."

Brody laughed. "You pose a pretty good argument."

"Just think of it as delayed gratification," she teased him.

He quirked a dark eyebrow and then, after quickly touching his lips to hers one final time, he released her from their tight embrace.

"Okay," he agreed as he slipped his hand into hers. "You've convinced me."

Willa cuddled against his arm as he led her toward the front door of the houseboat. Brody opened the door, stepped outside and then turned back to face Willa, his hand still intertwined with hers.

"I'll pick you up at seven." Excitement brightened his

features.

"Can't wait," she said as she moved to give him a kiss goodbye. But as she did so, she noticed that Hayden was standing at the far end of the jetty, nearest the houses, talking to a slender, professionally dressed woman with a short dark bob.

Brody followed her gaze. "What's Hayden doing talking to Carmody?"

It was something Willa wondered about herself.

TAMMY MANNERSLY

# CHAPTER FOUR

"Oh my God! Is that Brody Nash?"

The outburst came from yet another excited female fan. A portly middle-aged woman in a navy skirt suit and her slightly younger, skinner friend hurried over to where Brody and Willa were walking hand in hand along the Circular Quay waterfront, after their dinner at The Rocks. As he had all of the seven other times, Brody stopped, greeted the women with a friendly smile, signed what was offered to him and posed for photos.

Willa struggled to get over the strangeness of it all. Even though her grandfather was a high-profile movie director, she'd never had anyone rush over to greet him, as most of Brody's fans had done that evening. When she'd questioned Brody about the difference, he'd explained it was because directors, writers and the like weren't in front of the camera and therefore not as obvious in the public eye. Whereas actors, their entire job revolved around being on screen and so they were often more easily recognizable.

It made sense, but Willa still needed some time to adjust. It wasn't every day strange people ran up to the man you were falling in love with to tell him that they also loved him.

As Brody wrapped an arm around the older woman and posed for yet another photo, Willa thought back to earlier in the day when they'd noticed Hayden and Carmody talking. The two had frozen, wide-eyed, like deer in headlights when they'd realized that Brody and Willa were watching them. Then Hayden had smiled, waving a little nervously, before diving off the jetty and swimming back to his yacht.

Appearing less fazed, Carmody had smoothed a hand down her floral dress and approached. When she'd reached them with a glittery white grin, both Willa and Brody had immediately asked her how she'd managed to get down to the private waterfront area. They knew that only people who lived or stayed in the few mansions along the coastline of Point Piper were able to access the private jetties and pontoons adjacent to them. When Carmody had admitted that Brody's agent, had organized a key for her to access Brody's place in order to ensure things had been ready before his arrival, Willa felt uneasy. Something didn't sit right in her gut about the woman, probably the way she looked at Brody – as though she wanted to devour him in one bite.

Willa's eyes connected with Brody's as he posed next to the taller, skinner woman and he offered her a wink. She grinned. Even though Willa was desperate to have him back by her side, she didn't really mind sharing him with his admirers, as long as his love remained only with her. As Brody smiled once again for the camera, Willa remembered how quickly he'd asked Carmody to return the key to his mansion. It had taken both women by surprise. Willa felt secretly pleased by Brody's decision. She'd been troubled by Carmody coming and going from Brody's place without his consent, not just for security reasons, but because she didn't like the possibility of Carmody coincidently appearing in the vicinity when *her boyfriend* was deciding to take a shower.

Willa giggled to herself. *Her boyfriend.* It sounded so

adolescent, as though the two of them were in high school and talking about who's taking who to the prom. But, that's exactly what Brody had said when the rather nosy, blonde waitress had asked before seating them for dinner. He'd grinned at Willa as though daring her try to correct him. Of course, she hadn't.

When he'd said it aloud to the waitress, Willa's heart had skipped a beat. It was exactly how she'd felt. There was something about him that made her heart swell in her chest and her blood run hot with lust, need – and love, if she was honest with herself. Willa knew it was too early, she had only just met him, but she felt as though she already knew him more deeply, more honestly than she had ever known Hayden. It was terrifying and intoxicating Brody was quickly becoming everything to her and she just hoped that he felt the same way.

Brody waved goodbye to the women, who chatted amongst themselves cheerfully as they headed away, and then moved back over to Willa. As he reached her, he slipped his arms around her waist and pulled her to him.

"Jealous?" His voice was playful, jovial as he bent his head to cover her mouth with his.

Willa murmured a distracted, incoherent reply as her hands went to rest on his strong shoulders.

He ended the kiss, but left his lips close to hers. "Sorry, what was that?" Again, his tone was teasing. "I couldn't hear you through the lip-smacking."

Her eyes narrowed and she nipped at his lower lip. "If you're not careful, there won't be any more *lip-smacking* tonight."

Brody made his expression serious. "Okay, I'll behave," he told her, then laughed.

Willa chuckled as Brody ended their embrace and slipped a warm hand into hers. Enjoying his warmth in the cool night air, she snuggled closer to him as he led her over to a bench beside the harbor's dark water. They sat silently, holding each other. Utterly relaxed, Willa moved to lay her head on his shoulder, but stopped as he turned to look down at her. His expression was serious.

"I hope you know I'm falling in love with you," he told her, his voice rich and velvety.

Willa swallowed. She wanted to say the same thing, but was suddenly nervous of actually admitting it out loud and messing things up.

"I just thought you'd want to know," Brody continued, "in case you want to head for the hills and escape the craziness that is my life—" He motioned to a couple in the distance who'd obviously recognized him and had aimed a camera their way. "Before things become even more serious."

Willa swallowed again before brushing her lips against his. "It's already serious," she said softly. "I'm falling in love with you, too."

Euphoria filled his features and warmed her heart. If that wasn't a sign they were on the same page, Willa didn't know what would be.

Brody touched his full lips to hers in a long, slow, sensual kiss and Willa felt other, more sensitive, parts of her melt. Eventually, he pulled away just enough to gaze down into her eyes. His expression appeared suddenly curious and amused.

"Do you want to do something special with me next Thursday?"

Willa frowned. "With you? Do I have to?"

A smirk curved her lips as Brody chuckled.

"Some reps from Esquire magazine have flown out to do a photoshoot with me and I'd really love to have company."

She quirked a golden eyebrow. "So, I'm basically coming for moral support?"

Brody nodded. "Yep, that and I need someone to get me coffee."

In a playful motion, Willa slapped his chest lightly, but Brody just shrugged.

"What? You make really good coffee?"

She glared at him and the humor in his eyes turned to deep affection.

"And maybe I also want an excuse to spend more time with you."

Willa smiled a little smugly. "You don't need an excuse," she told him lovingly and then captured his soft, delicious lips with hers.

*

Brody smiled to himself, he just couldn't help it. He was pretty sure the smile hadn't moved from his lips since he'd heard Willa say she was falling in love with him. It was all he could think about over the last week, when they'd spent time together and when they hadn't. Even when he was supposed to be working, practicing his lines and getting into the mind of his new character, he was thinking about Willa.

Their romantic night at The Rocks beside the Sydney Harbor Bridge had been another incredible opportunity for them to open their hearts to each other. It still surprised him how keen Willa was to get to know him better and how much she wanted to support him in everything. Where had this woman been all his life? Had he finally found the perfect someone who would accept and love him just as he was?

Brody sighed deeply and his smiled widened.

"What's wrong with you?" Carmody looked up from the pile of papers she had been looking through.

It was Wednesday afternoon, just over a week since Brody's intimate dinner with Willa, and Carmody had come over to ask for some more signatures. One related to a company that wanted to add Brody as a brand ambassador, while the other was the final sign off on the agreed version of questions Esquire was allowed to ask for their magazine article. Carmody had sat opposite him at the dining room table as he'd scribbled his name next to each pink post-it note and was now double-checking that he'd signed on every dotted line.

"Are you coming down with something? I can head to the pharmacy if you need?"

Brody laughed and straightened in his chair. "No, thanks. I'm fine. Just happy."

Carmody's artificial grin returned. "Well, you've got plenty of reasons to be. You've got the Esquire shoot tomorrow and, chances are, they're going to crown you the sexiest man alive."

Laughing again, Brody shook his head. "I'm pretty sure there are lots of other front-runners for that title."

She shrugged. "Well, I know who I'd pick." With a wink, she leaned forward. "Want some company tomorrow? I know those photoshoots can be a real drag. I could always entertain you between shots?"

Brody shook his head. "Sorry, but I've already convinced someone else to come along with me."

Carmody's smile faltered and her expression hardened. "Willa?"

Brody nodded. "I hope she won't find it too boring."

Lowering her gaze, Carmody flicked back through the paperwork in front of her. "She wouldn't have been my first choice," she murmured.

Brody narrowed his gaze. "Pardon?"

Carmody shrugged again and then offered him an innocent smile. "Oh, nothing. It's just, you know, she seems…flighty, like she's got a problem focusing on one thing at a time. A bit like attention deficit disorder. But, whatever, I mean, she probably can't help it, you know…with all her commitment issues. I just don't think she'd be the one I'd pick to sit and wait quietly."

Brody chuckled, but it was a sharpish sound of disbelief. "I don't know where you're getting that impression," he told her.

Then he remembered how he'd seen her having a

heart-to-heart conversation with Hayden the other day.

"Look," he began again, trying to explain, "I'm not sure what Hayden told you, but Willa's nothing like that. She's told me about her commitment issues in the past, but it has less to do with her personality and more to do with not being true to herself and not being involved with the right person."

Carmody's left eyebrow rose as though in challenge.

Noticing it, Brody sighed, tired of her company and her behavior.

"Carm," he said, doing his best to make sure his tone was full of reassurance, "you're assistance while I've been here has been invaluable. You've done a fantastic job filling in for Kevin, since he couldn't be here himself and I'd love for us to continue working together, but you have to know that *nothing* is going to happen between us. You're beautiful, you're savvy and you're intelligent enough to know you're better off hedging your bets on some other guy than wasting any more energy on me. Okay?"

Brody watched her closely, waiting for her to either shrug it off or scream the house down, but she did neither. Instead, her eyes narrowed on his.

"What makes her so special?" Her voice was calm, emotionless.

Brody's grin returned as he thought about all the things he'd come to love about Willa.

"Well," he breathed, "she's just amazing. She's fun, smart, and witty." He laughed as he thought about how they teased each other, how much he enjoyed the playfulness of their relationship, even though it could also be so sincere, so real. "She's got her own life, her own goals. She's driven and passionate and wants to make her own way in the world, a bit like me. I love her honesty and how much she cares. She values me, not the characters I play, but the real me."

He let out a deep, satisfied breath as he stared into Carmody's impassive eyes. "There's just so many things really. I'm not sure anything really *makes* her special – she just *is*, to me."

Something flickered in Carmody's hard gaze, but Brody couldn't quite tell what it was. Annoyance, maybe? Or resignation? He hoped it was the later.

The corners of her lips quirked in a jaded looking smile before she glanced at her watch and then back down at the papers in front of her.

"Guess we should get back on task. I have a manicure appointment at three."

\*

Willa jogged down the tree-lined sidewalk toward her grandfather's mansion. The pink and purple hues of the diminishing sunset added a moody atmosphere to the street. She noticed a familiar car parked in the driveway. Even as she thought to turn around and head back the way she'd come, Hayden opened the car door and stepped out. He waved and offered her a broad smile. Seeing no other option, Willa continued on her way and slowed to a walk just before she reached the white Porsche Cayenne.

"Evening," Hayden crooned as he propped himself casually against the side of the tall, expensive vehicle.

Willa's hands went to her hips defensively. "What are you doing here?" She tried not to sound accusatory.

Streetlights were flickering on automatically, like glowing orbs in the darkening street.

"I wanted to ask you to go out with me tomorrow. I thought we could take a drive up into the Blue Mountains."

She frowned. "Rather last minute, isn't it?" She couldn't hide the suspicion from her voice.

Hayden's face contorted as though he was offended by her remark.

"I was having a crappy Wednesday at work, so I asked for Thursday off. There's nothing wrong with wanting a mental health day, Willa."

She crossed her arms over the colorful spandex of her exercise crop top, slightly annoyed and also surprised by his defensive tone.

"Is that what it is? A mental health day?"

Hayden shrugged and then smirked. "Maybe."

"It must be nice to have a boss that's so understanding," she told him guilefully and then quirked an eyebrow. "How is your father doing these days?"

Hayden's smirk widened. "He wishes I'd have less mental health days, focus more on the business, marry you and have lots of babies."

Willa chuckled. "Sounds like nothing's changed."

His expression became a little more somber. "Except us."

With a tired sigh, Willa dropped her arms to her sides and headed past him to the keypad in front of the tall iron gate which guarded her grandfather's property.

"I can't go with you tomorrow," she told him firmly. "I've got other plans."

She blocked his view, typed in the security code and then glanced back at him as the gate rolled open. He'd moved away from the car and had crossed his arms over his chest, crinkling the fabric of his light blue shirt. She could appreciate how attractive he was, but the feelings were no longer present. Their moment together had passed and it was time for Hayden to move on to someone new.

He tilted his head in the direction of Brody's mansion. "With him?"

Willa nodded. "He has a photoshoot and wants me to tag along."

The huge gate thudded to a stop and paused as though waiting for further instruction.

Hayden frowned. "You can't trust him, Wil. He's not good for you. I've heard things about him, things you wouldn't like."

"Like what?" Willa couldn't help but scoff.

She had been waiting for Hayden to fight back, to accuse Brody of bad behavior and make out he wasn't good enough for her. He'd done the same with the few guys she'd tried to date since they'd broken up.

Looking solemn, as though breaking the news to her was somehow difficult on him, Hayden shook his head.

"He's a cheater, Wil, a womanizer. Just ask Carmody."

"Carmody," she spat the name out. "I'm pretty sure she's got her own motives in all of this."

Hayden shrugged. "Probably, but I had to tell you. You needed to know the truth."

Suddenly exhausted, whether due to the exercise or the direction of the conversation, Willa took a deep, calming breath and stepped over the threshold and into the confines of her grandfather's property. As though reflecting her change in mood, the last colors of dusk dissipated and the sky darkened with the shadows of night. When she turned back to face Hayden, the large gate shifted, having been triggered by her movement, and slowly began to close.

"Go home, Hayden," she told him, more weary than indignant. "I appreciate your intentions, but you don't know the first thing about the real Brody Nash. You don't know him like I do and Carmody doesn't either. I know you want to protect me, but Brody's not someone I need protecting from."

Hayden's eyes grew wider as his gaze flicked between the closing gate and Willa, who was now standing on the other side of the decorative iron bars. He opened his mouth to speak, but Willa quickly cut him off with a wave of her hand.

"Go home, Hayden," she said again, her voice sounding tired and flat. "I hope you have a lovely mental health day tomorrow."

Turning on her heel as the gate locked into place, Willa headed down the driveway toward the mansion's front door. Even though she heard Hayden call her name and felt his gaze burning into her back, she didn't turn around.

# CHAPTER FIVE

Was it wrong for her to feel so turned on during a professional photoshoot? Seeing Brody pose in all of the outfits the Esquire crew had organized for him to wear had made her almost drool. How was it possible for him to look so damn attractive in clothes that seemed familiar – a leather jacket, a black-tie suit? Of course, there had been the topless swim-trunks sequence and another where he'd been wearing only a kilt in honor of a Scottish character he'd acted in a movie the year before. That had definitely excited her libido a little too much. But the main thing that heated her blood in all the right ways was the private look he kept giving her between shots. It was a mixture of love and desire. Every time he looked her way, it set her heartbeat racing. She wanted him and she wanted him bad.

As she watched Brody walk away to get changed for the final time, back into his own blue shirt and black jeans, Willa remembered how this morning, he'd literally picked her up, lifting her feet off the ground and then twirled her around with excitement. She'd giggled with glee and felt once more like a lovesick teenager. There was something about him that always had her smiling, and filled her heart with happiness. Willa had always known she was a woman who needed time alone to rejuvenate and steady her mind, but she didn't seem to feel that way with Brody. Being with him put her at ease, so she no longer needed that time to get back into her own headspace and on track. It was just one thing she loved about him, something that proved to her that maybe they were meant to be.

Willa had decided to bring up the conversation she'd had with Hayden the night before while they drove into the city. She had broached the topic more for herself than for Brody. She'd wanted to let him know that she trusted him. Strangely enough he'd explained to her that he'd had a similar conversation with Carmody. The conversation between the two on the jetty a few days ago seemed to make more sense to them. It appeared Carmody did have her own ulterior motives and was doing her utmost to split them up. Even though Brody had told her that he would speak further to Carmody about the entire debacle, he'd chuckled about the whole thing, which had made Willa laugh in turn. They seemed like two of a kind as though nothing could extinguish the love they shared together.

Willa grinned as she saw Brody re-enter the room. He gave her a knowing little wink which had her insides quivering, before turning to speak to the photographer. After shaking the man's hand, Brody headed over to her. Willa felt as though her face was splitting from her wide smile, but she couldn't help herself. She'd organized something special for them this afternoon and had been dying to tell Brody ever since she'd had the idea while eating dinner at her laptop last night.

"What's got you looking so pleased with yourself," Brody crooned to her as he grabbed her hands and pulled her up from the sofa she'd been sitting on and into his arms.

Willa giggled. "I've got a surprise for you."

His hands wrapped around her waist as hers slipped around his neck.

"Oh, yeah?" His deep voice was like silk as he cuddled

her closer.

"How do you feel about heights?" Excitement bubbled out with her words.

His gorgeous brown eyes narrowed on hers. "Why?"

She loved the playful suspiciousness in his tone, it only seemed to add to the thrill she was experiencing.

"Well," she began slowly, "I have a friend who works at Bridge Climb, the local company who takes people on tours of the Sydney Harbor Bridge. She told me they had a couple of spots open on the tour organized for this afternoon, so…I booked the tickets."

Brody's eyes brightened with enthusiasm. "Seriously?"

Laughing, Willa nodded. "Yes. We can head on over as soon as you're officially done here."

"I can't believe this." Brody held her closer, nuzzling his face into the sensitive skin of her neck. "I've always wanted to climb the Bridge," he purred against her skin. "Thank you."

"You're welcome." She relished the feeling of his lips against her throat. "I thought it might help you with your new acting part. You said you needed to be more spontaneous, more adventurous in order to help you understand your character's mind frame. Surely climbing four hundred and forty feet in the air might help."

Brody lifted his head enough to gaze down at her. Willa's heart leapt when she saw that his eyes were wide with surprise before they then softened with affection.

"You did that for me?" His voice was soft with disbelief.

She nodded, but before she could speak, his mouth claimed hers and seduced all remaining sense from her brain.

*

"This is unbelievable!" Brody's voice echoed before disappearing into the cooling air of the late afternoon.

He let out a howl of jubilation to the distant world below as Willa held him close and laughed.

"I take it you're having a good time then?"

He beamed at her and touched his lips to hers in a brief, but adoring kiss.

"You're incredible," he told her amorously before raising his hands out in front of him and motioning to the stunning view below them. "This whole experience is just the best!"

He wrapped an arm over her shoulders and hugged her against him as her hand slipped around his waist. Brody couldn't believe she'd arranged something so special, so unexpected for him. He couldn't remember the last time somebody had done something special for him without having an angle or getting something out of it for themselves in return. To think that Willa had organized it to help him with the difficulties of his current job made Brody's heart ache with love. She had already been so supportive with his new role, doing whatever she could to help him become like his character Mike 'The Wolf' Karver, but this was going above and beyond. She was making his dreams come true. Willa was the one for him, Brody knew it. He'd never really believed in true love, but his soul mate had come along and found him and now, he couldn't imagine living a life without her.

The wind whistled through the huge metal beams around them as they gazed down at the city below, taking in all of the sights and sounds from a new perspective. After they'd left the photographer's studio and the Esquire crew behind earlier in the afternoon, they'd driven to the Bridge Climb headquarters below the Harbor Bridge to begin their adventure. Willa had teased him when they'd slipped the blue, black and grey jumpsuits over their clothes and clicked the safety harnesses around their waists, saying she'd never seen a more attractive man in an onesie. Then he'd kissed her again and she'd completely forgotten her train of thought. Brody loved that he could do that to her, make her reality melt away.

Once they'd been prepped for the climb and had been told what to expect, they'd headed out and started their journey. Brody had been excited by the thought of it all, but when they'd actually begun walking, taking step by step up the monstrous structure, it had been everything he'd imagined and more. He'd let the feeling sink in, washing over him as he tried to envisage doing daring things like this every day, things 'The Wolf' would be prepared for at a moment's notice if things weren't going his way. Willa had been right. The experience, the adrenalin rush had helped to give him a new perspective and he was suddenly, finally feeling more confident about his upcoming role.

Brody glanced down at Willa, still cuddled against his side and he wondered: where had she been all of his life and why hadn't he met her sooner? As though sensing his stare, she gazed up at him, her big beautiful amber eyes bright with exhilaration and adoration. Reaching out with his free hand, he brushed a blonde curl from her face and let it fly away, over her head in the breeze. Damn, she was beautiful. That peaches and cream skin and those luscious lips were enough to have his mouth watering. He wanted to taste her everywhere and he didn't know how much longer he'd be able to keep those desires under his control.

"Smile."

The sound of Teagan's voice had them both spinning around to face her. She was Willa's friend, the Bridge Climb employee who had helped her organize this last-minute adventure and was just as Willa had described her – a bubbly ball of fun who adored heights and treated all her friends like family. Even though they'd only met a short time ago, Teagan was cracking jokes and playfully teasing Brody like any good sister would. With her petite build, dark curly hair and sparklingly hazel eyes, she actually reminded him so much of his own sister, Yvette, that he'd taken to her just as quickly as she had to him.

Teagan's own smile was wide as she held up a small

digital camera and waited for them to pose. Brody hugged Willa against him again as she did the same and he knew, without even looking, that their euphoric grins matched perfectly.

"Gorgeous," Teagan agreed.

She pressed a tiny button and the camera made a dull beep sound as it took their picture. They both watched as she looked at the screen on the back of the device and saw her smile broaden.

"Okay," she said, glancing back up at them, "now for a couple of silly shots."

After a round of photos involving peace signs made with fingers, tongues poking out, an attempt to 'hold' a building in the distance in the palm of their hand and a sweet shot of them kissing, Teagan showed them the results before finally moving on to another couple.

"Eternal memories," Willa teased as her gaze drifted from Teagan back to him. "That one of us with our tongues out is definitely a keeper."

Brody laughed. "Yeah, one to show our grandkids."

Although she chuckled along with him, the nervous look in her stunning amber eyes made Brody wonder if she'd recognized the sincerity in his voice. He hadn't been kidding. It was a special moment, something he wanted to share again with his family, with her family and maybe one day with their own.

Instinctively, his arm moved around her shoulders, just as hers slid around his waist and they pulled themselves closer into the warmth of each other. When Willa rested her head on his shoulder, letting the delicious scent of her, a mixture of soap, jasmine and something that was uniquely and exquisitely her own, waft around him in the breeze, Brody couldn't help but place a tender kiss on the top of her head.

She giggled again, less nervy this time and more contented. "What was that for?"

He moved his face so that his lips were against her ear.

"Come home with me," he told her.

It hadn't been a question, not quite a command, not even really a request. He'd heard the pure need that had filled his words, the hope, the lust, the love.

When she didn't answer straight away, he'd known she'd heard it, too.

"I'll cook," he offered.

Glancing up at him, away from the extraordinary view of the city, she smiled. "Is that a bribe?"

Brody smirked. "You wouldn't ask if you'd ever tried my cooking."

Willa laughed. "Okay, I'll come home with you – if we can cook together."

He narrowed his gaze, his eyebrow quirked up with suspicion.

She just shrugged. "I figure if we put our terrible cooking skills together we may be able to make something at least partially edible."

*

"You know you can leave that," Brody told her, his brown eyes glittering with humor as he watched her drag the huge pot into the soapy sink.

"What? For the cleaners?"

He shrugged. "Yeah. Or the dish-washing machine."

Teasing him, Willa held her chin high. "Unlike certain famous movies stars I know, I do my dirty dishes myself."

Brody laughed. "I was just trying to give you an out," he explained as he motioned to the inside of the pot with the dishtowel in his right hand. "That cheese looks pretty burnt on."

Willa tried to scrape at it with a plastic glove covered finger and then frowned.

She'd enjoyed the traditional feeling she'd had when she'd first slipped on the pink rubber gloves a little while after dinner and suggested they wash up together. It had added a sweet normality to their relationship. Down the road, she could see them doing the same thing, even though Brody's life was anything short of ordinary. It made her hope for something she'd never really put much thought into: a long life with someone she loved. Even though they'd only known each other a short time, it seemed like a natural progression, and she was actually looking forward to the idea.

"Look, I'll promise not to make fun of you if you decide to give up and leave it." Brody held his hands up, the dishcloth around one, as though in surrender.

Willa eyed him warily. "You think I'd give up that easily?"

He shrugged, but his mocking smirk was a declaration of war.

Snatching up a handful of bubbles, she took a deep breath and blew them at him, sending soapy white clouds up into the air and in the direction of his face. With a deep laugh, Brody moved quickly and extinguished a few bubble bombs with a wave of the dishcloth, but missed the higher couple that landed on his forehead. When they touched his skin, Brody's eyes rolled upward as though trying to see the extent of the damage. An uncontrollable giggle burst from Willa's lips. The mischievous promise in Brody's gaze had her own eyes widening and then she squealed with excitement and little bit of playful terror as she dashed off toward the living room.

"It was a total accident," she giggled over her shoulder as she ran.

"I don't think so." Brody's velvety voice held a lilt of menace causing Willa to move faster.

Glancing back, she managed to skip out of reach, just as he made a lunge for her and put the long, cream-colored sofa between them.

"You were supposed to be cleaning the dirty dishes, not me." He purred threateningly.

Willa shrugged as though unfazed, but shifted from

foot to foot anxiously, prepared to run off again at any moment.

"Maybe you had a dirty mind?" She touched her forehead, pointing to herself to show where the soapsuds had landed on him.

Brody brushed at the puffs of white soap which remained on his skin. "You know you'll have to pay for that?"

The teasing tone in his voice had her heart racing in anticipation. She forced her expression to soften innocently. "Me? Obviously, it was my evil twin."

Brody rolled his eyes. "Obviously."

She nodded. "And, so I shouldn't be punished for something *she's* done."

He seemed to poise himself, muscles tightening as though he was just about ready to pounce. "I think that this time, we can make an exception."

When he lunged toward her, she squealed again and ran, but just wasn't quick enough for him. He snagged her around the waist and dragged her onto the soft cushions of the sofa. She giggled as they bounced, then Brody pulled her beneath him and knelt above her. Grinning roguishly, he grabbed her hands in the damp, pink plastic gloves and raised them over her head to rest on the soft sofa arm. With his free hand, he tickled her ribs through the lavender-colored cotton of her blouse. Willa giggled and squirmed, then almost got her hands free before his grip altered and tightened, holding her still in place. She laughed so hard, her stomach hurt.

"I'm too ticklish. No. I can't take it," she giggled as his hand moved to her stomach again.

Brody's wicked grin darkened slightly as his gaze raked over her torso. His hand lowered over the fabric of her blouse, just below her belly button as his fingers popped open the button there. As the warmth of his skin met hers, a breath caught in her throat.

"Are you ticklish here?" His voice deepened throatily

with desire.

She nodded. "Yes."

He chuckled as his hand slipped beneath the material to stroke gently over the bare skin of her ribs. "And here?"

She murmured her agreement and then bit her lower lip. All the fight had now drained from her. Even though his hand still held hers securely above her head, she wasn't about to try to escape. It all felt too good, his strong hands on her skin, the supported weight of him resting on her thighs, the heat of his body so close to her intimate core. Her insides turned molten as electricity tingled from his fingertips through her veins, turning her nipples hard and melting the sensitive spot between her legs.

"How about here?" Brody's fingers snuck just below the rim of her lacy bra to draw a delicate line under her right breast.

Her answer was almost a moan. She watched him lick his lips, his dark eyes focused hard on her own as his hand moved beneath the fabric to cup the supple mound. Again, her breath caught and her head fell back further into the sofa cushion. As his fingers found her nipple, lightly pinching the peak, her gaze met his again. He stared down at her for a little longer, the look of desire and longing in his eyes making her heart swell, before he bent his head to press his lips to hers.

The touch of his mouth was light at first as he lowered the hard line of his body to rest against the smoothness of hers, but it quickly became fervent with each chaste taste. He nipped at her lower lip and then devoured her, tongue plundering, dancing with hers, then licking her teeth, her kiss-swollen lips. As he pressed himself against her, the hard length of him restricted by the denim of his pants, she opened her own jean-clad thighs to him and moaned as the heavy pressure of his solid erection hit its target.

Feeling the hand around her wrists loosen, Willa slipped free of his grasp, quickly dispensing with the pink rubber gloves before letting her hands roam over his body.

They glided under his shirt, up along his muscular back and then down to clasp around the rough material covering each perfectly rounded butt cheek. Brody groaned as his hips rocked against hers, pushing himself into the heat of her, and making her body ignite with greedy desire.

How had they managed to wait so long? Willa couldn't comprehend it. She knew she'd wanted to wait, wanted to get to know the real him before they took things too far, but now her lust for him seemed insatiable. She felt as though she was burning from the inside out with the painful yearning, the ardent hunger she had for him.

As Brody's fingers caressed her body, covering one breast then the next and moving behind her back to unclip her bra, Willa's hands snuck between them, tugging at his belt buckle and then his fly. She yanked his blue shirt over his head while he completely freed her of her lavender blouse and the crumpled mess of her lacy brassiere. When his lips found her pert nipple, she gasped. He suckled there, teasing her with his tongue, while her fingers stroked through the silk of his dark hair. Brody kissed a line up her skin to her throat and back down the other side, capturing her other breast with his mouth. A small cry caught in her throat as his teeth nipped at her skin and then she couldn't help it anymore, she was grabbing at him, pulling his mouth to hers. Willa kissed him, ate at the sweetness of him while she tugged at his pants, at hers. Brody laughed into their kiss, surprising Willa in her haste and making her smile against him.

"What?" Her voice was husky and desperate with passion.

Brody chuckled again, then kissed her, sucking at her mouth, making her mind and body melt. His grin was wide and delighted when he finally paused to let her catch her breath.

"I think you're my *one*, Willa. I think you're *it* for me."

A heavy, contented throbbing began in Willa's heart,

matching the throb of desire building, pounding at her core. It was a blissful feeling, sending a surge of warmth throughout her entire body.

When Brody's lips found hers again, deliciously consuming her, and her hands continued their plight, tugging at his pants and then hers, a silent reply echoed through her mind, and etched itself deep into her soul: *I think you're the one, too.*

# CHAPTER SIX

Even though it had only felt like a short time to her, Willa was pretty sure that a whole day and a half had passed since their little intimate incident on the sofa, then the living room floor, before eventually making it to the bedroom. There they'd stayed for hours and hours, discovering each other, and only leaving for the necessities like food and water, and even then, clothing had been optional. It had been heaven, an idyllic dream. She hadn't wanted it to end, even though she knew they had to get back to reality at some point. But, as Brody had told her, they could spend every night this way for the rest of their lives.

She should have been terrified. A commitment like that was constricting, limiting and unspontaneous, all things she'd never been fond of, but with Brody it just didn't seem that way. She was looking forward to the future with him. It was an unusual feeling for her, but oddly satisfying. He just made her so happy, and fulfilled her in no way she'd ever experienced before.

Turning off the faucet, Willa stepped from the shower as steam wafted around her in the large, white-titled bathroom. She released a long, satiated breath and then shook her head. She'd been sighing constantly ever since Brody had left at ten that morning to meet up with his personal trainer, Tim. It was the weirdest thing, as though her body was trying to find a way to release all the pent-up happiness she felt, without having Brody there to share it with.

After drying herself off and wrapping the fluffy blue towel around her middle, Willa sighed again and then moved into the bedroom to find her clothes. Seeing the wrinkly material of her blouse lying unappreciated on the light grey carpet, she remembered she had meant to head down to her houseboat to grab new clothes before her shower. Absentminded as she was at the moment, she shrugged and searched the room for something to wear. In a top drawer, she found a white t-shirt and navy boxer shorts and decided to slip them on until she could find something better or be bothered to head back to her place to get something new.

While it was a tempting thought to snuggle back under the covers and wait for Brody to return, shower and join her, Willa's rumbling stomach had other ideas. After heading out into the upstairs corridor, she skipped cheerfully down the eggshell-white marble staircase. When she'd made it to the bottom, she attempted a ballerina twirl on the shiny, slippery surface of the ground floor before stumbling with a giggle. She felt like she was sixteen again and had just been asked out on a date by the popular boy she'd had a crush on since eighth grade. Willa laughed out loud to herself at the thought and the sound echoed joyfully down the large corridor before her.

A dull thudding sound answered her and had her freezing in surprise. It had come from a room at the end of the long aisle, probably the kitchen, but that shouldn't have been possible, she was supposed to be alone.

"Hello?" Willa called out warily, but started to wonder if Brody had come back earlier than expected.

A smile spread her lips as she thought of him drinking

a cold glass of water at the sink, all hot and sweaty with his strong muscles glistening and flexing as he moved. Butterflies flittered around in her stomach from excitement. Her cautious pace quickened as her libido kicked in and she hoped he'd come back early to surprise her. Wouldn't he be amazed if she were the one to appear beside him instead?

Stifling another giggle, Willa finally reached the kitchen, but stopped dead.

Dressed perfectly as usual in a snug mahogany-colored dress, Carmody leaned her curvy hip against the large, white marble island in the center of the room. Her black briefcase was propped beside her, while her hands rested on the stack of paperwork she'd spread around on the countertop. As their eyes met, she offered Willa a sharp smile.

"Did I wake you?" Sarcasm dripped from her words like venom on the fangs of a viper.

As anger began to overwhelm her initial excitement, Willa stalked into the room. "What are you doing here, Carmody?"

Carmody raised her eyebrow and then she tilted her head. "I have a key."

Putting herself between Carmody and the door, Willa's hands went to her hips and she felt her features harden in annoyance. "Brody told you to return that. This is his place. You don't have the right to come and go as you please if he doesn't want you to."

A dark eyebrow rose. "Who says he doesn't want me to?"

Willa felt her jaw drop. "Are you deaf or are you just stupid? I was there on the jetty when he told you and that was well over a week ago."

A sardonic grin pulled at Carmody's red lips. "What he says in front of you and what he really means are two different things?"

Crossing her arms over her chest defiantly, Willa let out

a catty chuckle. "I was wrong on both counts. You're not deaf or stupid, you're just crazy."

Carmody straightened and stepped away from the marble island, moving menacingly closer before halting just in front of Willa. Being nose to nose would have felt intimidating if Willa didn't already tower above the haughty brunette woman. Carmody's russet-brown eyes narrowed, her dark brows furrowing, creating deep wrinkle lines between her eyes.

"You think you know everything, don't you, sweetie?" Her condescension was like a physical blow.

Willa smiled, mockingly. "Well, I definitely know Brody better than you do."

Carmody let out a sharp scoffing sound. "Don't be ridiculous. I'm as good as his agent while he's in town. I know everything about him, do everything for him. He tells me things he would never even consider telling you."

It was Willa's turn to jeer harshly at the absurdity of Carmody's announcement. "I think it's time you realize something, Carmody." She pointed her index finger at the other woman's chest. "You're just a filler. You're only needed while Brody's agent is still overseas. You're just an extra pair of feet, extra hands. You're a lackey. You do what you're told and that's it. It's better that you come to terms with it now, instead of believing that you're going to be single-handedly supporting a big client like Brody when he heads back to Hollywood."

Carmody's mouth widened as though in shock and then her expression darkened with anger.

"He doesn't care about you," she spat, retaliating by pointing a finger of her own. "He's never really cared about you. He only got to know you because I told him about your grandfather, about how it would be a good chance to network if he got in big with someone like Murray Stone. That's the only reason he's wooing you, the only reason why he's screwing you. Once he gets the meet and greet with your grandfather, the ultra-famous director, he'll drop you like yesterday's garbage."

She revealed her perfect pearly white teeth in a contemptuous snarl.

Willa rolled her eyes. After her discussion with Brody the other day, she'd been certain Carmody had been doing her best to split them up and this proved it. Brody had been honest with her about her grandfather the first night they'd opened up to each other, there had never been any secrets as Carmody suggested. Willa just couldn't believe how low this woman would go, especially since she couldn't see what Carmody was getting out of it? Did she want to kick Kevin out and be Brody's one and only agent? Or was she interested in a more intimate affair? Either way, Willa was certain Carmody wouldn't be getting anything she wanted. Brody had already expressed his distaste of her numerous times, explaining that the only reason he continued to keep her on the payroll was due to the fact that Kevin had been right, she was a brilliant personal assistant and excellent at PR.

Even though anger still burned inside her, Willa felt sorry for Carmody. She may have been a stuck-up, obnoxious man-eater, but she was still a woman who was fighting for something she wanted dearly.

Willa's hands dropped from her hips and her expression softened with pity. "Look, Carmody. I know you care about Brody as a client. If it's me you're worried about, that I'll somehow hinder his career or get in the way, then you can stop right now. I'm here to support Brody one hundred and ten percent. I want him to achieve his dreams and he feels the same way about me. I'd rather help you than fight with you, so if having a key to his place is something you need to help organize things with him, to help you do your job better, then we can figure something out. It might unsettle me, but what matters most in this is Brody. It's his place and if it helps him and his career, then I'm all for it."

Carmody's features remained firm as she seemed to

analyze Willa's expression, but then they faltered and relaxed.

"I don't need your pity," she said, sounding more exhausted than irritated.

With a tired sigh, she turned on her heel and headed back to the paperwork on the top of the kitchen island. As she gathered it together, she glanced back up at Willa.

"Having a key is useful," she began, "but not necessary."

She opened her briefcase and snatched out a colorful yellow keychain. She tossed it across the countertop toward Willa, the metal of the key and the keyring tinkled together on the smooth surface before hitting the designer fruit bowl near the edge.

As Carmody gazed up again, a tight grimace creased her facial features making her look much older than her twenty-something years.

"I know that you think you and Brody have something special." After a sigh, she shrugged her limp shoulders. "Maybe you do. Whatever. I guess I was just worried about how that would affect his career. You know, sex appeal does a lot for an actor when they're single, but if they've got a partner, things can get more...difficult." Frowning deeply, she shrugged again. "It doesn't matter."

Willa's brows knit together and her stomach ached. She'd never thought about how her being with Brody could actually hurt his career. *Surely it couldn't; could it?* Willa swallowed. She knew of plenty of actors who had partners or were married and still kept their A-grade status, didn't she? She tried to think of some, but only came up with a list of divorcees. There was a lump in the back of her throat she couldn't quite swallow.

"What do you mean?" Her voice yelped out, sounding as though she was in pain.

Carmody turned and leaned her hip against the counter. She watched Willa cautiously and then bit her lower lip, looking suddenly anxious. "I shouldn't be telling you." Her hands clasped together nervously. "Please don't tell Brody, not yet. I have to find a way to tell him."

"Tell him what?"

Willa's heart was pounding. The thought that something terrible enough to affect Brody's future could have had something to do with her, had Willa absolutely terrified. How would Brody ever forgive her when he found out? She wasn't sure whether all the love in the world would be enough to keep them together if she'd been a part of the reason why Brody had lost his meaning in life.

Carmody's face was sullen as she shuffled through the papers in front of her before pushing a document across the countertop toward Willa.

"That role he's been practicing for," Carmody's voice had risen in pitch as though it hurt her to speak, "the character he's committed to, that he's been doing everything he can to become...well, the company, they have rescinded their offer."

Willa's jaw dropped and she lunged for the paperwork that had been passed to her. "They can't do that! Everything's signed."

She stared down at the document. It was a letter from the CEO of the film production company. It was all there in black and white, had the official letterhead of the company and was even hand-signed.

"There's a clause in the contract," Carmody continued as Willa read. "If they're afraid the choice of actor will greatly decrease their expected profit, cinema attendance, etcetera, the company retains the right to void the contract."

Only partially hearing Carmody, Willa read further through the document. Apparently, there had been posts on social media of Brody and his new love interest. Pictures of them at The Rocks and even shots of them together on the Sydney Harbor Bridge. Willa knew for certain she had never posted anything. Social media marketing may have been her job, but besides promoting her company, she wasn't really interested in having her personal life broadcast over the internet. As for Brody, she was also pretty sure if he'd been aware of the clause in his contract and the affect their relationship might have had on his career he wouldn't have posted anything either. That just left the fans they'd encountered during their adventures out together. At the time, Willa hadn't thought anything of the photos. Most were only of Brody or him and his overzealous female admirers anyway, but there had been a couple which weren't. She even remembered that they'd both agreed to let Teagan print one of the snapshots she'd taken of them on the Bridge to post up in the Bridge Climb lobby with all the other photos of celebrity visitors.

She gasped and covered her mouth with her hand. Her whole body shook.

"I can't believe this." Her voice came out breathy.

Willa wasn't usually a fainter, but she felt like one now. She placed a hand on the cool marble of the island and tried to breathe deeply, to calm her racing heart. How could this have happened? She had wanted to prove to him that he was capable of anything, that he already had all of the skills to be able to achieve what he wanted to achieve, he just had to stop doubting himself. But, instead, she'd ruined everything for him. Brody's greatest loss was her fault.

"I'm sorry," Carmody said as she gathered the paperwork and shuffled things back into her briefcase. "I shouldn't have told you. I just…it's going to be difficult to tell him. I'm not sure what to do."

Willa nodded instinctively, feeling suddenly distant as though everything around her weren't really happening for real. She handed Carmody the document and watched as she placed it inside the briefcase and then clipped it closed.

"I should go. I really shouldn't have told you." Carmody's words came out quickly as she headed for the door.

As she moved to pass her, Willa reached out, gently grabbing her arm. "I'm glad you did," she said.

Her expression serious, sincere, Carmody nodded and then left.

Willa didn't turn around, didn't move. She heard Carmody's heels clip-clop down the corridor, the front door open and then close. Time moved slowly around her and the air seemed suddenly thick and difficult to breathe in. Her limbs felt heavy, her body only supported upright because she'd leaned on the kitchen island. Her whole world was falling apart. She was about to lose the love of her life and she couldn't do anything to stop it. Brody would hate her, when she'd taken so much from him, been the reason for the destruction of his dreams. She could imagine how he'd feel when Carmody finally told him. She knew how she'd feel if she had been rejected due to something not quite in her control.

The solution seemed simple. If Brody had never met her, then he would never have ended up in this situation. Her leaving would be the best thing for him and that was what Willa was going to do.

Finally feeling strong enough to move, Willa walked out of the kitchen, down the corridor and out of Brody's mansion, out of Brody's life forever.

# CHAPTER SEVEN

The last thing Brody had expected when he'd arrived home late after an intense exercise session with his personal trainer was Carmody making herself comfortable on his sofa. He'd heard the noise of the television in the living room and had assumed that Willa would be lounging there waiting for him. He had been imagining a repeat of their intimate encounter on the cream-colored sofa as he'd quickly shut the front door and hurried inside. Yet, those thoughts had rapidly disintegrated when he'd seen another woman in her place.

Carmody rose to greet him, that perfect, but creepy smile pulling at the corners of her mouth.

"Did we have an appointment?" His tone was clipped as he moved to put a single chair between them. "I didn't realize you would be coming around today."

She shook her head and stepped closer. "Do I always need a reason to drop by?"

Brody's dark gaze narrowed. "Did Willa let you in?"

He glanced toward the ceiling, wondering if Willa was upstairs putting some much-needed distance between the women.

Carmody shook her head again and twirled a set of keys

on a blue keychain around her index finger.

"She's gone. Couldn't handle the heat. Guess it'll just be you and me from now on."

Brody's frown became savage. "Why do you still have a set of keys and what are you talking about – gone? Where is she? Where's Willa?"

Rolling her eyes, Carmody moved closer to him, but then became surprised when Brody hastened away.

"She wasn't good for you, Brody," she snapped. "I told you that."

He felt his lip quirk up in a snarl as he glared at her. "What happened, Carmody? What have you done?"

She released a frustrated sigh. "What makes you think I did anything? I told you she was flighty. She might have up and left you, just like that."

Brody's expression remained hard. "Carmody." He said her name through gritted teeth. "What did you do to her?"

Infuriated, Carmody tossed her arms in the air and stalked away from him. "What had to be done." Spinning around, she perched herself on the arm of the three-seater sofa. "You're better off without her. We'll accomplish more together than you would have ever achieved with her."

This time Brody prowled ominously toward her. "Carmody."

If she didn't attempt to explain herself, he would throw her outside on her ass. How had his perfect day ended up becoming the absolute worst? He couldn't believe Willa would have just left him, without comment or explanation. He knew she was scared of what they had together, but she was a communicator. She never would've left him without telling him why.

Carmody gave him a sharp sneer, curling her lips back from her teeth. "Why won't you give us a chance? Why won't you let us be good together?"

Brody's face contorted in disgust, but held his tongue. If he angered her now, he wouldn't get the answers he needed.

"Because we're not meant to be together," he told her. "I'm in love with Willa and nothing you do will—"

"I know, I know." Carmody cut him off with a curt wave of her hand. "I'm not good enough for you and never will be. The story of my life."

Her gaze had darkened, more with pain than with anger and Brody noticed the fury which had been brimming in him a moment ago was subsiding. He could see her now, the real Carmody and she wasn't exactly the person she portrayed. Just like he did when he was acting, she was playing a character, pretending to be or rather wanting to be someone she just wasn't. For some reason, she had let herself become a sad, lonely, desperate woman, when she really shouldn't have been. Even though she wasn't his type, Carmody had a lot to offer any future partner. She was attractive, smart, scarily determined and terrifyingly loyal. Maybe she just needed to realize that.

Brody felt his features soften as he gazed down at her. She had crossed her arms protectively over her chest and had tilted her head away from him petulantly.

"You've got to value yourself more, Carm." Brody forced his tone to become more sincere to help get his point across. "Just because someone doesn't want you in the same way you want them, doesn't mean that they think you're not good enough for them. Mostly, it's just because you aren't the right person for them. You need to find *your* right person, Carm. It will happen, but you can't force it."

Carmody glared up at him, her reddish-brown eyes full of anger and annoyance. She watched him carefully and then breathed out a sigh. Her gaze lowered as did her hands and she suddenly looked deflated.

"You're a bastard," she told him, her tone only slightly heated. "You should've chosen me."

Brody let himself chuckle lightly. "I'm just not the one for you, Carmody."

She sighed. "Whatever."

He stared down at her until she finally looked up at him again.

"Tell me what you did so I can fix it." It wasn't a judgment, just a flat statement.

Carmody rolled her eyes. "I may have implied," she sighed heavily as she waved a hand in the air, "that your relationship with her was negatively affecting your career."

Brody's brows furrowed in confusion. "What?"

Her expression became more innocent and she bit her lower lip. "Let's just say that with a little creative thinking and the use of Photoshop, I was able to make her think that the production company for your next film was dropping you because you were no longer single."

Brody scoffed loudly. "That's absurd."

"I was very convincing." Carmody smirked, looking much too triumphant for his liking. "I should've won an Oscar."

Dropping his face into the palm of his hand, Brody tried to gather his thoughts. How could Willa have believed such a lie? Obviously Carmody had given her enough evidence. He needed to find Willa and win her back before she left him forever.

Straightening, he hurried over to the closed French doors and swung them wide open. He glanced down to the neighboring pontoon where Willa's houseboat had been moored for the last few weeks, but it was vacant, there was no houseboat in sight.

He spun to face Carmody, who had turned to look over her shoulder at him.

"Where did she go?" He knew his voice was high-pitched, almost hysterical, but he didn't care.

Offering him a naïve expression, Carmody moved to shrug.

"Where?" Fury bled through his voice as he ran back to her. "Don't lie to me, Carmody. If you know something, you better tell me now."

Her hard gaze narrowed on his, as though in challenge

and she opened her mouth to answer, but nothing came out. She paused, her expression softening as though she was reconsidering her words. Then she groaned, sounding unhappy or irritated with what she was about to do.

"Hayden called. She's gone back to the yacht club."

Hope filled Brody and his dark eyes brightened with determination.

"Thank you," he told her as he moved quickly toward the corridor.

At the entrance, he stopped and glanced back at her. He felt a little sheepish doing this now, but it had to be done. Things had gone too far and they couldn't be taken back. "I'm sorry, Carm, but you know that I'm going to have to fire you."

Shrugging nonchalantly, she released a long-drawn-out breath. "I know."

When her russet-brown eyes met his again, Brody offered her a reassuring smile.

"I'll write you a good reference though."

She pretended to narrow her gaze threateningly. "You better," she teased before nodding. "Thanks."

Brody's small smile widened and then he was running, down the corridor and toward the front door. He had to tell Willa that everything was all right, that Carmody had lied, and that he – loved her. It may have seemed too early, but he needed her to know now.

*

"I'm not letting you through, buddy, so you can just get back in your fancy car and go home."

Hayden was like an impenetrable wall at the entrance to the Cruising Yacht Club of Sydney. It seemed obvious to Brody that Carmody must have called him when Willa had left his house and now Hayden was here to play guard dog.

"I need to see her, Hayden. Let me through."

Brody tried to control his frustration and keep his

anger in check, but his patience waned. If he didn't move his tall, blond ass from the front door of the yacht club in the next five minutes, Brody was going to see if he could put a dint in Hayden's perfect jaw.

"Sorry, but you're not a member, so you aren't allowed through."

Hayden's well-muscled arms were crossed defensively over his broad chest, but even with his aggressive stance he still looked preppy. It probably didn't help that he was wearing a white Lacoste t-shirt and beige chinos. Brody, on the other hand, still hadn't changed out of his sweaty gym attire. His crusty red singlet and knee-length, black running shorts probably made him look like a person not worth welcoming into the civilized environment of the yacht club.

"Who's not a member?"

The hoarse, masculine voice came from behind them, forcing Brody and Hayden to glance toward the opened door of the entrance.

An elderly gentleman with a neat white beard stepped forward. "Hayden, I saw you loitering out the front here and was wondering what—"

He paused as he reached Hayden's side and finally looked over at Brody.

"Is that?" Surprise brightened his features. "Hayden, that's Brody Nash!"

Hayden gave him a look which suggested he was in no way impressed, but the elderly man ignored him. As Brody smiled politely, the other man extended his hand in greeting.

"Mr. Nash," he said excitedly as Brody shook his hand. "My name is Bill Evans. I'm the President of the club here. Can I help you with something?"

"Don't worry about it, Bill, he was just leaving." Hayden smiled smugly at Brody.

Bill frowned. "Don't be silly, Hayden. That's not how we treat guests here."

With Brody's hand still in his, Bill pulled him toward the entrance.

Hayden's face contorted in shock and annoyance. "You wouldn't have even given him a second glance if he hadn't been famous," he griped.

Pausing in step, Bill's hand moved to pat Brody's shoulder. "Why don't you head on inside, Mr. Nash. I'll be just a moment and then I'll be in to give you the grand tour."

With an appreciative nod and excited by the chance of escape, Brody moved quickly toward the door. As he opened it and went to slip inside, he heard Bill and Hayden arguing.

"But, Bill, he's not a good guy. He—"

Obviously, Bill had cut him off.

"You're just like your father," Bill's throaty voice followed Brody inside. "Being a pompous ass might help you in the business world, but it doesn't make you friends."

Brody was grinning to himself when the door closed behind him.

Five minutes later, he'd finally figured out how to get onto the huge jetty where the yachts and Willa's houseboat were moored. But, as he ran down the narrow path, he noticed a familiar boat pulling away from its mooring.

Suddenly, he heard footsteps thudding behind him. Glancing back, he saw Hayden gaining on him, with Bill standing at the jetty's entrance gate, waving his fist angrily at Hayden. Bill seemed to be shouting, but his words were inaudible, Hayden's, on the other hand, weren't.

"You're too late," Hayden yelled, his voice echoing through the corridor of boats. "I've called her. She knows you're coming."

Fury fueled Brody, spurred him on, helping him run faster. If he wasn't so desperate to get to Willa, he would have headed back to Hayden and punched him in the face for being such a pain in the ass.

After he'd powered through a few more steps, Brody could see the vacant space, the empty, but disturbed water where Willa's houseboat had been moored calmly only moments before. As he glanced up and across the turquoise water which glistened in the bright sunlight, his gaze following the tiny swell created by the vessel's departure, he saw Willa's boat. It wasn't that far away and wasn't moving too quickly. In the gentle breeze of the beautiful blue day, he could hear the steady chugging sound of its motor.

Hayden's footsteps thudded closer. "She's gone. You can't get to her."

Brody had a brief moment where everything seemed to blur. He glanced back at Hayden, then back out to Willa's boat. He couldn't see her, but he knew she was inside there somewhere. He had to tell her now, he couldn't let her leave without telling her. The fear of losing her had him looking at the water. He could swim. He was a good swimmer and her boat wasn't too far away. He looked up again, focusing on the houseboat. He could do this.

"Willa!" It was a yell, a deep booming sound, which seemed to rise above the chugging of the deserting boat.

Then Brody was diving into the cool crispness of the salty water and using his strong arms to stroke powerfully through the small waves as he swam expertly toward Willa's home.

*

"Willa!"

The sound of her name thundering across the water had her turning off the motor. Had someone really called out to her? It had sounded like Brody, but it couldn't have been. Hayden had told her that Brody had arrived at the yacht club and because he knew she didn't want to see him and that she wanted to be left alone, she should probably motor away elsewhere for a while or so until he had the situation handled. Though she hated to leave Brody in Hayden's capable hands, she just wasn't ready to look into Brody's eyes and see the hatred, the anger, the betrayal. She didn't know what he would think of her after Carmody had finally told him what had happened, that he'd lost a role that was so important to him because of their relationship.

Willa felt the boat slow and float listlessly as she moved toward the back porch. She was sure the sound had come from behind her. It had sounded so close she wondered if someone else was already onboard. As she opened the screen door and stepped outside, she glanced around. She was a fair distance from the jetty now and she could see Hayden waving his arms around in the air. Maybe he had called out? Maybe he was trying to tell her it was safe to head back in. It did sound like he was yelling, but she was struggling to make out words in the jumble of sounds. She waved back, but wasn't sure what to do.

Remembering her mobile phone, she turned to retrieve it, only to be startled by the sound of something hitting the side of her boat. She hurried over, worried something might be doing damage to the vessel, when a wet, human hand slapped onto the deck and then a familiar face appeared.

"Brody?" Astonishment made her voice sharp and shrill.

He breathed heavily as he pulled his whole body up from the water and onto the deck. He was still dressed in the gym gear she'd seen him leave his house in earlier in the day, even his black running shoes, and looked completely haggard.

"Willa." It was an exhale of breath, barely a name.

She helped him stand and then pushed him toward one of the plastic chairs in her outdoor setting. When he was seated, she turned to head inside, thinking only of finding a towel to dry him off, but he grabbed her hand to stop her.

"Don't go," he told her, his dark eyes piercing into

hers.

Willa knelt beside the chair, keeping his wet hand tight in hers. "I'm here," she said. "Are you okay?"

He laughed breathily. "I think," he took another breath, "I need to add swimming back into my exercise routine."

She chuckled, but it was a short, abrupt sound and her grin didn't quite reach her eyes.

"What are you doing here?" Willa couldn't hide the fear in her voice.

She was so worried Carmody had told him, and he'd been so devastated by the news that he'd had to find her.

"What are *you* doing out here?" He smiled affectionately. "I thought you were going to relax at my place until I got back from training?"

Willa frowned and her heart sunk. Carmody hadn't told him. Did that mean she had to break the news? She felt her features furrow in concern and dropped her gaze to stare at their intertwined fingers.

Leaning forward, Brody reached out with his free hand and smoothed the lines of worry on her forehead with his cool, damp fingers. "Carmody told me about what she said to you," he began.

Willa's gaze shot back to his. "She did?"

Fear clouded her vision. Was he angry? Upset? She couldn't see anything like that in his expression. He just looked – content. His dark, cocoa-brown eyes were bright and his jovial grin was loving and tender.

"She did," he confirmed. "Willa, baby," he stroked a finger down her face, "it was all a lie. She made it all up. They can't void my contract just because I'm dating someone."

Willa's eyes widened. "But—the document!"

Brody shook his head. "Carmody told me, she did it herself, used Photoshop or something. It was all a ploy to split us up, like everything else she's done."

Willa stared at him, trying to analyze his face. Was he serious? Had she actually been nice to that woman, even felt sorry for her and then played right into her damn perfectly manicured hands?

Finally understanding the truth of the situation, Willa slapped a hand to her forehead and closed her eyes.

"I can't believe I was that stupid," she whispered.

She heard Brody chuckle and then his hand was under her chin, lifting it. Her hand dropped from her face and she gazed up into his beautiful eyes, so close now to hers. Brody grinned down at her.

"You're not stupid," he told her. "From what Carmody told me, she was pretty convincing."

"And then some." Willa nodded. "I think she should try her hand at acting."

Brody laughed and then pressed a kiss to her lips.

"Don't leave," he pleaded quietly.

Willa shook her head, brushing her nose lightly against his like an Eskimo kiss. "No," she agreed.

His gaze narrowed before he chuckled again.

"I think I finally understand," he said, grinning.

"Understand what?"

"That line that's been bugging me." He shrugged and then gave her a mischievous smirk. "*Life is only worth living if you've got something to lose.*"

Willa laughed. "You're only realizing this now?"

He smiled sincerely. "I guess I've never really been afraid of losing anything, until I'd thought that I'd lost you."

She grinned up at him, love swelling in her heart, adoration beaming through her gaze.

Brody's grin was infectious before he brushed his mouth over hers again. "I need to confess something," he said against her lips.

Instinctively, Willa felt herself jerk back a little bit. "Confess?" She didn't think it sounded good.

Brody nodded slightly as he slipped off the chair to kneel beside her, his clothes still dripping with water, creating a little puddle on the clean, white deck.

"I lied to you the other night when I told you that I was falling in love with you," he said, his deep voice becoming velvety soft.

Eyeing him suspiciously, Willa frowned. "Oh, really?"

He nodded again. "I should have said...I'm *in* love with you."

She felt the corners of her lips quirk upward as her eyes glistened with coming tears.

"I love you, Willa Stone," Brody told her proudly. "I'm pretty sure I loved you the first time I saw you, during your first break and enter attempt."

A laugh burst from her lips and she slapped him playfully on his cool, damp shoulder. "I thought you didn't date criminals."

A dark eyebrow rose as though in challenge. "You were never convicted."

She laughed again and wrapped her arms around his neck, pulling his body, wet clothes and all, against hers.

"I love you, too, Captain Famous, including your alter ego Brody Nash."

He laughed, sliding his arms around her waist and holding her against him. When his lips met hers again, Willa knew she wanted to be with him always. Their love for each other fulfilled her. They were meant to be, she was certain of it and she would never ever again let anything manage to come between them.

The End

The new doctor in town is attracting some attention, especially of the female persuasion, but art teacher, Erica Townsend is blissfully unaware until she ends up injured and in his office. Too bad she'd vowed to resist love—that traitorous emotion, the destroyer of lives—after numerous failed relationships. Something about Matt, about their electrifying connection has her wondering if he might just be...*the one.*

Dr. Matthew Garrick is tired of playing wing-man for his best friend. It isn't that he wishes to look for love, rather the opposite. But the eagerness of some of the single women in their small country town unnerves him. That is, until a certain stunning brunette appears in the waiting room of his medical practice. Her touch sparks something deep inside him, jolting his heart into a new rhythm and Matt makes it his mission to win's Erica love.

Can he convince her to take a risk on him and what they share together?

As the good doctor strives to show Erica that love doesn't have to come at a price, his dangerous secret admirer threatens to prove otherwise.

*Whoever said love wasn't dangerous?*

# Now Available at all Major Book Retailers!

Swimming superstar, Sebastian DuMont, agrees to headline the reopening of the Poseidon's Shore Health Club at a discounted fee, grateful for an excuse to visit his beloved hometown. However, he hadn't expected to be tempted by the lovely Zenia, owner and operator of the fitness facility.

All of Zenia Andino's dreams come true with swimming superstar, Sebastian DuMont, attending her gymnasium's reopening. She'd idolized him as a teenager with his poster pinned to her bedroom wall, but meeting the hunky celebrity in person gives her heartbeat an excited new rhythm.

Before they can test the waters, Seb's agent interferes and Zen's fame-hungry sister alludes to an affair with the Olympian. Will Seb keep up the lie for continued fame and fortune? Or is it finally time to follow his heart and feed the special spark he felt with Zen before the opportunity extinguishes forever?

# Grab Your Copy Today!

*You can't hide from destiny....*

Callum Hawthorne is one of those lucky guys who seem to have it all. He's a wealthy property tycoon, the CEO of his family's company. He's handsome, intelligent and charming and has a gorgeous new woman on his arm every week. But there's one thing still missing – the love of his life, Lucy Spencer.

Fourteen long years ago, Lucy left for college and cut off all contact with Cal, leaving their mutual friend Madison as his only connection. That was until in his effort to save his deceased father's beloved Gold Coast property, The Calypso, Cal contacts Insight Marketing, the best advertising firm in Melbourne, and discovers his Lucy among the team.

Successful marketing executive, Lucy Spencer had managed to avoid her ex-best friend for nearly half their lives. Fearful of trusting him, loving him and having her heart broken all over again, Lucy tries to keep her distance from him, but discovers that there is a fine line between love and hate, and maybe – just maybe – Cal could be her inescapable destiny.

# ~Persuading Lucy, a 1st Place WINNER for the prestigious 2018 Chatelaine Book Awards for Romance Fiction, will quickly become your new favorite read.~

*Invited by one brother, tempted by the other...*

Former Australian playboy Blake Davenport knows his billionaire brother, David, is capable of anything to ensure he gets what he wants. But manipulating his young daughter's beautiful teacher into marriage is unacceptable.

Gwen Deveraux is grateful for the invitation to spend Christmas and New Year's with her beloved student's family, especially when her handsome host is so eager for her company. After surviving a broken heart, she is finally ready to give love another chance.

*But, who with?*

The illustrious David Davenport whose real motives seem hidden behind charm? Or his roguish brother, Blake, who has tempted her heart and body from the very moment they met?

# Now Available at all Major Book Retailers!

# ABOUT THE AUTHOR

Tammy Mannersly is an Australian author based in Brisbane, Queensland. She loves writing romance, has a fondness for animals, is crazy about movies and enjoys a great Happily Ever After. Her passion for writing started from a very young age and led her to complete a Bachelor Degree in Creative Industries majoring in Creative Writing at Queensland University of Technology.

You can find out more information about Tammy and her work on her website: www.tammymannersly.com or by visiting:

Facebook: https://www.facebook.com/tammymannersly

Goodreads: https://www.goodreads.com/author/show/16935790.Tammy_Mannersly

Instagram: https://www.instagram.com/tammymannersly/

Twitter: https://twitter.com/TammyMannersly